The Other World

The Other World

Tales from Southern Hemisphere

Madhumita Thakur

PARTRIDGE
A Penguin Random House Company

Copyright © 2016 by Madhumita Thakur.

ISBN: Hardcover   978-1-4828-6738-1
            Softcover   978-1-4828-6737-4
            eBook   978-1-4828-6736-7

Print information available on the last page.

To order additional copies of this book, contact
Partridge India
000 800 10062 62
orders.india@partridgepublishing.com

www.partridgepublishing.com/india

Contents

Acknowledgments

Writing a book had been my long-time dream and perhaps a much cherished desire ever since I developed a love for words. And yet the journey of writing this book has been the most daunting experience of my life. Every day when I sat to pen down my thoughts my hands would freeze and my mind would get filled with a strong sense of self-doubt and fear.

I must have given up on my dreams countless times and had it not been for my dearest husband, Ajeya Arakala, I would have never accomplished this feat. He believed in me when I didn't believe in myself and constantly encouraged me to think beyond my fears and take that ultimate leap towards realising my dreams and becoming a novelist. His unflinching love and unreasonable faith in me helped me sail through all odds.

Apart from him, another major contributing factor towards completion of this book has been Australia. This country is where my hobby for writing turned into my profession allowing me an uninhibited start towards doing something I had been passionate for long. It will be unfair on my part to not thank all of my clients across Australia, US and India who have presented me with various opportunities to hone my writing skills and keep pushing my own boundaries outside of my limitations.

Not to forget all my dearest friends who have constantly provided me with their feedback for each piece of article penned down by me and kept suggesting that I should write a book. My desire indeed got reinforcement from each of their statements.

I am also extremely grateful to Mr Achintya Bhattacharya and Mrs Kanu Bhattacharya, for showering me with their blessings, love and faith when I needed it the most.

I could not have accomplished all of this without being loved and blessed by my mom and my dad and without the constant motivation and support from my sister and my brother. They are the backbone of my existence and their contribution in my life is beyond any definitions.

Last but not the least I also want to thank each of my reader for posing their trust in me and showing the courage to give a first time author like me an opportunity to tell them a story in my own unique way.

Prologue

'Lee's birthday'—it was an event reminder flashing on my phone for some time now, but the laziness of the Saturday morning hadn't permitted me to take a look at it before.

'Is it 4 November already?' I asked Avantika, still in my sleep, but got no reply. Then I slowly moved my right elbow towards her to nudge her a little bit, thinking she too must be asleep, but my elbow couldn't locate its target. There was absolutely no one beside me.

She must have gotten up early, I thought to myself and went back to snooze for some more time. Avantika was my wife, who loved the early mornings, especially the weekend mornings. I often teased her, saying that while the rest of the world loved to sleep in the morning she liked to get up and don the hat of a superwoman.

My cell phone beeped again, so I had to get up now. I opened my sleep-laden eyes and looked around. I grabbed my phone from the bedside table and silenced the alarm. It was Lee's birthday reminder. Reading that message took me back down my memory lane. I made a mental note about calling up Lee later in the day. It was an annual ritual which Kris, Lee, and I had been doing for several years now, and it had kept us bonded to one another strongly through the fading impacts of time.

'Sushant, are you up?' Avantika entered into the room and gently shook me by my feet. I opened up my eyes and looked at her. Although I hated the fact that she was trying to wake me up, I loved how careful she was while tapping on my feet.

'Oh yes, I am up. It's Lee's—'

'Birthday today. Yes, I remember.' Avantika completed my sentence even before I could do so. She looked at me with a smile, which has always been very reassuring for me.

'Let's have some tea now. I have made your favourite ginger tea. Then you can freshen up and call up Lee.' Avantika walked out of the room without even waiting for my response to her proposal. She knew if she gave me an option, I could sleep for a few more hours.

I got up and stood in the balcony. It was a balmy morning, and the city's commotion hadn't assumed its ugly form yet. I found it soothing to watch the world go by from my balcony. Of late, it had become like a relaxation mantra for me, especially when I coupled it with a cup of ginger tea made by Avantika. She had magical hands. I had always been an ardent fan of ginger tea, but I had never guzzled it the way I did after tasting Avantika's version of it. After a good long stretch, I started watching the commotion of cars and people move on the road with equal zest, and I could not help but think how important it was for drivers as well as pedestrians to make the right judgement call at the traffic junctions. No matter how careful one is, the uncertainty about other driver's behaviour can never be discounted. It could destroy everything for someone in a minute.

Choosing a specific path in one's life can be very scary, especially when, as a teenager, you are standing clueless at life's juncture and every juncture appeals to your mind with equal lust and success. The whole world appears glossy yet full of contradictions and self-doubts, particularly through the rose-tinted glasses which people, especially from my generation, choose to wear. You may feel you know your mind, yet there's this lingering feeling which raises your heartbeat and trickles down a few drops of sweat on your temple.

It is often the fear of the unknown which drives us to choose what we choose, but are all unknown things really bad? Is choosing something completely against your perception and belief system a sign of a weak mind?

What was the right path for me? Will I be able to find success and live my dream? These were just a few questions battling in my head when life threw me at an important juncture almost a decade ago.

And while there was no set way for me to find out the answers for these questions with 100 per cent certainty, I relied upon my instincts to nudge me and guide me in that direction.

What unfurled later changed me and my life forever, and this is just my way of sharing those experiences with you and taking you down my memory lanes where the story of my life began to unfold.

Chapter 1

The Harbinger

I was born into a family which was obsessed with studies, education, degrees, and everything else which could potentially revolve around it, just like the whole of India is completely fixated to Bollywood, cricket, and religion. In India, the first two fixations are stronger than any religion and collectively have more followers than any one religion individually boasted of. And my life also kick-started on a similar note—not Bollywood or cricket but studies. Many people found this combination quite surprising as it just did not go along with our stereotypical traditional image. After all, we are Gujaratis, and business, not education, was supposed to run in our genes. We inherit the penchant for dollar, just like a child inherits the basic DNA of his parents, and our hearts inevitably beat in sync with the volatility of the stock markets. However, I had everything different in my life starting from this point onwards.

After a perfect schooling and a perfect grooming, I entered what is expected to be the best phase of a person's life—college. I was not particularly a handsome boy back then, but I still managed to turn a few heads in my direction. After all, who doesn't like to look at a boy who has noodle-like curly strands and a thick black-framed eyeglasses sitting on his nose? I was no less than a hero, although in my own world with my own USP (ultimate style and power). Now, before you get more inquisitive about my style and power, let me clear your misconceptions that I did not possess either of the two attributes. Rather, I was a simple boy with average academic interests, but I could never figure out why my look was so nerdy. Maybe both my parents had deeply desired for a baby who would be Einstein's clone, if not his reincarnation to say the least. But I didn't look like him either. Sometimes I thought I resembled Malinga (that Sri Lankan cricket player who could easily nest a few birds on his head) more than I did my parents. Sometimes I also wondered if I was adopted by my parents from some downtrodden adoption centre where a hapless soul might have left me wrapped up in a piece of cloth. Anyway, why am I sharing all this with you? I wanted to tell you about my story—the story which transformed my notions about life on the other side of the world.

This is about that time when I was in the second year of my college. New year and new session had just started. Our generation was sitting on the cusp of computer era, and Internet was riding high on the technology wave. If there was one thing which people from my generation were certainly good at, it was the social know-how of computers. And when I say that, I don't mean being good at just the computing languages or the networking stuff related to it. What I mean is being expert at using computers for literally living their lives on social networking websites, endless chats, uploading their pictures clicked in all possible ways to appear cool and happening, and so much more. Google and *Wikipedia* were considered more knowledgeable and bankable than the real books by our generation for any information.

I didn't have girls drooling over me, and neither did I have any expertise in dealing with them, but when it came to computers, I was no less than Mr Bill Gates. Oh, maybe that explained my nerdy looks! Not that Mr Bill Gates was a nerd, but then if it weren't for him, I would not be sure what our entire generation would be doing. Going back to Bill Gates, he might have taken the world by storm when he created Windows for computers, but unfortunately, it was not him who was Mr Fix-It in my college. From professors to students to clerks, everybody depended upon my help and quick fixes for their computers and online issues, including the IT department of our college. Books never interested me. I was a man of practices, quite literally, except that I was still a boy.

Anyway, on that fateful day when I reached college, I was summoned to the principal's office around break time. I was sure our principal's old haggard desktop must have broken down again. It was not the first time he had called me to his office. I had fixed his computer at least half a dozen times in the last two months. Although there was nothing majorly wrong with his desktop, the fact that it ran on 8085 processor (or something which was as ancient as that) dampened my enthusiasm to fix it each time.

On many such occasions, I had secretly wished to destroy this computer to finally put an end to the era of dinosaurs, but alas! Dinosaur was the public secret of our college which signified our love–hate emotion for our principal sir's computer. It surely didn't match up to the dinosaur in terms of size, but I am confident that it would have been a strong contender in terms of age. It generally took anywhere between thirty to forty minutes to boot up each time, and I dreaded that moment when I had to shut it down while fixing.

'May I come in, sir?'

'Ah, Sushant! Come in, my boy,' our principal sir said while scanning me from top to bottom. I don't think that my appearance conjured up a good impression especially with my tucked out shirt and my hands over the bag straps on my shoulders. I immediately put down my hands and entered his office.

'You know why I have called you here?' our principal sir said this with a strong voice he often used to create a sense of fear as though I might have done something wrong.

'Yes, sir,' I instantly said while still trying to figure out if I had indeed broken any of his stringent rules.

'Yes? What do you mean by yes?'

'Sir, your computer—'

'Shut up! Students like you have no sense about how to talk to their teachers, leave alone to the principal.' He said this almost fuming at me, but all I could focus on were his irregular-shaped teeth splashed with red spots and black streaks. Although we have never seen him biting, chewing, or relishing any form of those granular-powdery things in tinges of white and brown, we had a feeling that he survived on it for all his obnoxious villainous traits. I wondered if, within the privacy of his home, he idolised Gabbar from the *Sholay* movie to draw all his inspirations and ideas to keep the students threatened by him. Maybe someday I should follow him stealthily and get a glimpse of his cave. I was almost certain to spot the big pictures of villainous characters like Gabbar, Shakaal, and Mogambo proudly hung up on his walls in thick black wooden frames.

'Do you understand that?' I suddenly came out of my detective ploy and realised that our principal sir was still belching out his frustrations on me.

'Sushant, I am talking to you!' he barked yet again.

'Yes, sir. I understand it completely,' I murmured even though I had no idea what he was expecting me to understand.

'Good! You are an intelligent boy, and I have some good news for you,' he finally said with a smile on his face, although I was still glued to his tainted teeth. His teeth were like magnet for my eyes. No matter where I looked, my eyes were ultimately getting pulled towards his rather colourful teeth.

Has he upgraded the dinosaur's processor, or did he get a new computer? My mind was racing faster than his speech, and I was exploring all possible reasons which could indeed be a piece of good news to me.

'You know our college has an exchange programme with some of the best universities of the world.'

'Yes, sir, I am aware of that.' *But how can that be good news, especially for me?* I thought. Agreed, I was a computer-fixing guy of our college, but my academics were clearly no proof of that.

'You have been selected from our college to go and study in Melbourne University for the next one year.' Our principal sir said this while exhibiting his set of pearly white teeth which were not so pearly or white any more. I am sure that if it were possible to accommodate more teeth in his mouth, then he would have flashed those as well. I had never seen anyone with that wide a smile.

'So pack your bags, my boy.'

'Yes, sir,' I said with not much enthusiasm in my voice. I was least expecting anything like this in my life, and mentally, I was not prepared for it.

'What happened? Are you not happy with this news?' our principal sir asked with some concern in his voice.

'Of course, sir, I am happy. I am just a little surprised,' I replied. I don't know why, but I was being honest to him.

'Well, but I am not. Everybody in our college knows that you are a genius in the field of computer. So what better opportunity can you find than this to gain some international exposure and learn more things in your field of interest?'

He had a point.

I had never seen this aspect of our principal sir's personality till date, and now I was wondering which was more shocking—the news of my international study or my princi's thoughtful words. Our seniors had coined a term *princi* for him, which had gradually become the most preferred way to address him by everyone and was used at all times when he was not around. It was weird how well this name reflected our different feelings each time, whether we joked, got angry, felt frustrated, or even said nasty things about him. It was a one-stop solution for the entire college whenever they felt the need to sum up their emotions for him.

'I understand that you had not expected such an opportunity to knock on your door. But now that it has come, you must grab it with both your hands. Think about it over this weekend, and let me know by Monday morning. If you are not happy to participate in this exchange programme, we can select someone else. Remember that time and tide wait for none.' Princi murmured this while arranging some papers on his desk and looking at me through the corner of his bespectacled eyes.

'Thank you so much, sir.' I said this looking at him while my mind felt numb and frozen.

'You can go now, and don't forget to inform me on Monday.' Our principal sir had said his final words on this topic.

'I will, sir. Good day.' I left his cabin after saying this. I was feeling quite confused after that meeting. While I was happy that I was being offered such a wonderful opportunity, I was also jittery about leaving my old friends (making new friends), my food, my lifestyle, and other things about my life which I had not thought about before. Time was flying very fast. This was possibly the worst weekend of my life, except the ones where I had to study for my exams. I never had to think so much about something, and this made me feel totally perplexed and overworked. It was already Sunday, and I was still in the same state of mind, so I thought of doing some online research on this Melbourne University.

I also thought of taking advice from my parents on this particular topic, but I was almost definite that if they come to know about this exchange offer, they would surely ask me to take it up—even that wouldn't have been a trouble. Trouble would have begun after that, with my mom advising me on what to do and what not to do in a foreign country.

Somehow, she believed that anyone who went to a foreign country becomes a joint-smoking hippie with long hair, guzzling alcohol and, yes, sleeping around with the white girls, or becomes too materialistic with a plush house, luxurious car, and world-class facilities but devoid of relationships and emotions. Truth was she feared I would get westernised, and she clearly didn't want me to become that. She was a well-educated lady, but the few incidents which she had come across in her life had tainted her opinion on living life in a foreign country for good. I knew she wasn't completely correct, but I didn't have the patience to explain things to her.

Anyway, so while my mom would fill me in with such rigmarole, my dad would preach me over how to be penny wise and spend money only when required.

Both my parents were well-known professors in different universities, and they excelled in their jobs, but somehow, I could never understand this aspect of their personalities. My agony would generally start when they would bring their professions straight into my life—preach and lecture—and try to drill something or the other into my head every other day. So I had decided that I would inform them about this opportunity only if I wanted to go down that line. I was going crazy thinking about this offer. I had not felt so pressured to make a decision in a long time, so I thought of doing some research myself in order to ease out some pressure and use the Internet to help me take a call. After all, we didn't keep chanting '*Jai Google Baba*' for nothing.

I sat on the computer and started browsing through various websites to get some reviews on the university and the courses which were included in the exchange programme. I have to admit that everything appeared very alluring—the sports, the leadership programmes, the social and networking opportunities, the competitions, and of course, the promise of world-class education. The more I read, the more I was getting convinced about accepting the offer. I was convinced that I was going to experience something very different, something very unique, and I did—just not what I had thought it to be.

I wondered, after all, how difficult would it be to live in Melbourne? I knew how to speak English. I could make new friends there, see new places, meet new people, and actually live the lifestyle of the world's best city. That's what the Internet had informed me by far.

The image which had conjured up in my mind was so exhilarating that I instantly knew what I had to do. I smiled at the computer and wondered if I could ever get any better friend than that. It was my friend, guide, and philosopher all wrapped up in one, especially when I really needed one. Other times, it would stay shut and not bother me with anything additional. It also respected my privacy and understood that every person needed some me time and lots of space.

I spent the rest of the Sunday evening dreaming and beaming with excitement, although my parents didn't appear to take notice of it. They had no clue that in a few weeks' time, they would be getting transformed from worldly-wise professors to a set of hysterical parents every child in the world seems to have.

Next morning when I woke up, I was feeling very light and fresh. I quickly got up from the bed, got ready for the college, and told my mom that I would eat something for breakfast either on my way to the college or in the canteen. I didn't want to waste more time at home eating breakfast, so I waved at my parents and left a bit early that morning. As I stepped out of the house, I could hear the distant but shrill voice of my mother asking me to at least carry a banana.

We had some ground rules at home, one of which was about not stepping out of the house on an empty stomach, especially in the morning. I knew they would get very annoyed with me, so I came back and grabbed a banana from the fruit basket kept at the dining table, although I knew what was coming along in its fate.

Adolescence is that phase in our lives when we do not care if something is right or wrong. All we care is if something is easy and fun to do or not.

I usually took a bus ride to my college from a nearby bus stand, which was just ten minutes away from my house on the days when I walked. That morning, I was walking towards the bus stand, and I could feel the spring in my steps. I had heard that guys generally have this kind of bounce in their walk either when they are in love or when they take the phrase 'Become all things to all men' too seriously and practically. I was glad I did not fall in any of these categories. Maybe it was the music playing in my ears through my headphones which was doing this magic, and with Jagjit Singh's velvety rendition of a ghazal in '*Hosh walon ko khabar kya*', I thought it was totally possible. I still couldn't figure out if my liking was stronger for Jagjit Singh's voice or for the ghazals, or if I was plainly mesmerised by the concoction of both of these elements.

I looked at my watch. It had just been five minutes since I had left home when suddenly I heard a splashing sound around me. Before I could fathom what was happening, something forceful came and hit my face. Within seconds, my face was drenched with rainwater accumulated in the potholes from last night's unannounced rain. Without even batting an eyelid, the auto driver swung his auto and skilfully drove away like a horse on a road as though nothing had happened. I was left to my own amusement and fate to tackle this dirty situation. I instantly checked if my T-shirt too had borne the rants of this disgruntled driver because, unlike what the advertisements say, '*daag achchhe nahi hote hai*'. I was relieved to find out that my T-shirt had escaped this morning wrath of drain water, but I still had to clean my face. I checked my pockets for a handkerchief but just couldn't find one, so I rummaged my bag.

Even amidst so much dirt and stench, a smile broke on my face when my hand caught hold of my handkerchief. Maybe this is called the joy of small things. I wiped clean my face very hard so that all dirt and stains get wiped out in one go. I felt my face with my hand, and after feeling satisfied with the result, I walked ahead, along with cursing the culprit (the auto driver). Thankfully, my bus arrived on time, and I managed to get inside it despite the heavy rush and my bad mood. Not that I ever got bothered with the frequent stares and second looks from onlookers, but today, I was praying to God to let those stares and looks not be there for embarrassing reasons.

Within fifteen minutes, I reached my college, and I was glad that there was no drama during my travel time.

I went straight to our principal sir's office just to find out that he had still not come. My lectures were about to begin in another five minutes, so I was not sure if I should wait there or go back for my class. But then good sense prevailed upon me, and I was convinced that the option of waiting for our principal sir was far more interesting and worthwhile than trying to appear attentive in a class where the professor himself didn't know what he meant when he said 'Phlot the last phart of the graph'. This professor was an ardent fan of our politician Didi from Poshchim Bangla. His life's biggest tragedy was his inability to articulate the difference between the sound of *p* and *ph*, and consequently, he never realised how *parts* used to transform into *pharts* into his class. I also never understood what went inside my other professor's head when he blurted sentences like 'Hey, you bottom two, stand up' or 'Hey, you front two, come here'. What began as bouts of laughter slowly settled with my sighs and wishes of RIP to the world's most influential language.

I had heard many people killing English with their self-created dictionaries of words and pronunciations, but this one cracked me up completely. While most of the backbenchers in my class managed to giggle, the front-row students were forced to keep a poker face in all kinds of hilarious situations. Those who couldn't agree with the poker face would just pretend that either they were getting asthma attacks when such incidents happened or just looked down at the floor as though they had found their calling in the centre of the gravity.

Nevertheless, I must have looked at my watch at least over a dozen times in the last five minutes. In a little while, I saw our principal sir coming from a distance, so I got up and quickly checked my T-shirt, my face, and my hair to straighten out any signs of the morning tragedy which had struck me with vengeance.

'Good morning, sir,' I wished him as he approached his cabin.

'Good morning, Sushant. Come after five minutes.' Our principal sir said this without even looking at me or waiting for any reaction from my end.

'Okay, sir,' I said in a low voice and sat back on the bench outside his office.

I waited for exactly five minutes and then entered his office. Whatever happened after that was not new to me. I had rehearsed this conversation many times in my head (and in front of the mirror too) since Sunday, and everything went exactly like that.

'I am glad that you have made this decision, Sushant. I respect it and hope that it will pay you off very well in shaping up your career.' Our principal sir said this to me with a beaming face, and all I could think was *Damn! This man knows how to smile.*

'Thank you, sir,' I replied to him.

'I will email you the details of the course and Melbourne University by the end of the day today, and tickets will be given to you in a couple of days by one of our staff members.'

'Sure, sir. Thank you once again for this opportunity.'

'No problem, my boy. Do well there. Now go and start packing your bags. Melbourne is a cold place.'

'Yes, sir. Good day,' I said and left his office. I wanted to share this news with everyone, so I immediately updated my Facebook status to 'Melbourne, here I come'. Despite the fact that all my friends were attending lectures, there were ten likes for my status message and about a dozen comments, all asking the same questions of what, when, and why. And of course, there was the obvious one: 'Dude, party time.' Now it was not hard to figure out which of these comments were posted by my female friends and which were posted by my male friends. Had it not been for these smartphones, the number of students attending each lecture would have been considerably less in any college. With most of the phone companies providing free access to multiple apps and social networking sites, nobody really bothered about sitting in the boring lectures for hours. In fact, they kept themselves entertained by circulating the eccentricities of each professor or lecturer, and I have to admit that I too contributed in popularising some of the famous antiquities of our professors.

I decided to skip the rest of my lectures that day and go straight to my home. I was too excited, and I wanted to enjoy this feeling amidst the array of gadgets and technology in the comfort of my home. I shared this news with my parents when they got back home in the evening, and as I had expected, my mom started with her share of preaching, followed by my dad's sermon on becoming penny wise. Luckily, I had trained my mind to switch off in such situations, which were perceived as SOS signals by my brain.

I transported myself to Melbourne in the meantime and started exploring its proverbial winter. Everything appeared white, snowy, and glamorous. A bunch of fair-skinned girls wrapped up in micro-miniskirts and knee-length boots appeared immaculate and alluring.

A sense of freedom dawned upon me as I explored Melbourne in my mind. I could wear what I wanted without my mom's interruptions. I could roam around in the city as long as I wanted without being tracked by human GPS systems like my parents. I could grow my hair long and even sport a ponytail. And lastly, I could be far away from my nosy neighbours, meddling relatives, and the maddening crowd who often make you realise that we are indeed a country of over a billion people.

'Sushant! Are you listening to me?' I heard my mother's loud voice and thus ended my reverie for the day.

I packed and repacked my bags several times until both my parents were satisfied that I had taken everything considered immediate and urgent by them in all conditions. They had checked with my USA-based relatives about things which were allowed to be carried overseas. It included everything from a Boroline cream to ready-to-eat packs of *thepla*, *gathiyas*, and *khakhras*, recipes to prepare home-made buttermilk, and dozens of other stuff. While I could relate most of these things to my parents' lineage, what baffled me were the years of fascinations of my parents for Boroline. It somehow did not justify our Gujju connect, but didn't I tell you right in the beginning that my life has always been a little different in all aspects? Maybe this was just one of those things. I just shrugged my shoulders and checked my bags one last time.

I looked at my tickets and thought that by this time tomorrow I would be in Melbourne. I couldn't wait any longer, so I started dreaming about it, albeit this time on my bed, tucked comfortably under my blanket.

This was going to be my maiden overseas trip alone, and more than me, it was my parents who were nervous and filled with trepidations about how safe and comfortable I would be on my own. My concerns were more around the big black Samsonite bag, which appeared monstrous to me with its forty-kilogram weight, and the image of my thin frame lifting that suitcase didn't quite seem convincing. I was almost certain in my mind that either I would not be able to lift my bag from the baggage claim section or I would not be able to identify which bag belonged to me, especially after I had vehemently ordered my parents not to put any name sticker on my bag. Little did I know then that, by the end of my trip, both of my fears would be proved wrong—far, far away from being true.

I reached the international airport in the evening well on time along with my parents and began hobnobbing at the airport for my airline counters. My parents seemed more than happy for me. After all, their highly academic and distinguished family was going to see another family member receive accolades, although computers were totally an unexplored subject till now in my family. A long queue stood like a landmark for the counter we were looking for, and I couldn't help but wonder what could possibly make people travel far, far away to an island country at this time of the year even though I knew mine.

While we were waiting in the queue for our turn to collect the boarding pass, a rather random person walked up to me and asked me what my full name was. I looked at his suited appearance and thought he might be some airline official, so I showed him my passport and gave him my full name, after which he disappeared from there. I was fairly certain that the purpose of gathering my details would be to perform a drug scan on me during the security check. Not that I was being cynical, but I couldn't see any other reason for the airport authorities to come and ask me my name just out of blue. Anyway, when the line moved ahead and it was my turn to collect the boarding pass, the lady behind the counter looked at my passport and informed me that I had been upgraded to the business class. 'What?' I blurted out to my father.

There must have been some mistake. I was sure I hadn't heard it right. Sensing my confusion, the lady at the counter once again confirmed that I was booked in for business class. Since there were some vacant seats in the business class and since I was one of the few well-dressed people amongst the passengers queuing up, they chose me for the upgrade. I was certainly ecstatic, but more than me, I could see my parents beaming with joy. Somehow, it comforted them to know that I would be covering the longer leg of my journey in the business class rather than an economy class, and I was overjoyed for the obvious reason.

Like they say, well begun is half done, so I took my upgrade to business class as a sign for all good things which would come my way in Australia. After collecting my boarding pass and making sure I actually got a business class ticket, I bade goodbye to my parents with teary eyes and a very anxious mind.

Month 1

Chapter 2

Tryst with Reality

Everything went smoothly, and after about two hours of wait at the airport and twelve hours of flight travel, I finally reached Melbourne.

This would be a new chapter in my life, I thought to myself after landing in the airport of the world's best city and walking towards its baggage claim section. This was my first trip outside India, so I was a bit jittery. I went straight to claim my baggage before making calls to my parents about my safe arrival. After about twenty minutes of wait and a few rounds of bag exhibition, I finally saw my black bag. I couldn't have missed it in any case because my daddy dear had pasted a big piece of paper on it with my name and other details written in bold and capitals despite my strict instructions of not doing so. I quickly grabbed my bag, kept it on the trolley, and made my way out to the exit before anyone else could spot my name and other details from the other end of the airport.

I clearly remember my first impression of Australia. My first experience of Australia was that of Melbourne's Tullamarine Airport (of course, back then, I was completely oblivious to the existence of other airports like the Avalon). I got busy scanning Tullamarine to gauge what this city and the country would be like. It was then that the magnanimity of the Melbourne Airport struck me with its absence.

This was the first blow to my golden dreams which I had weaved tenderly for days together before coming here. I couldn't believe what my eyes were seeing.

Whoever had said that first impression is the last impression couldn't have been more wrong in this particular instance. The tinsel image of Australia which I had conjured up in my mind for weeks not only got smashed, but it also left me wondering if this is how developed countries look like—boring architecture enclosed in the most unpretentious space.

'Is this really Melbourne?' I said aloud to myself, and after looking at the signboards and listening to a few announcements, I was sure that I was at the right place, although mentally I was still at loggerheads with my own imaginations. There was no gloss and no jazz which could make me feel that I had come to a developed country. I felt unwelcomed and almost cheated by Karan Johar. I wanted to sue him or, even better, hack his computer—that would perhaps be the best way of taking revenge on him. Although I was in a state of shock, my mind was simultaneously trying to remember any Karan Johar movie which was shot in Melbourne or Australia, and it turned out in vain. Maybe I shouldn't have cursed that poor fellow after all. He had just over-glamorised the lives and worlds of NRIs, but everything that I thought I knew about Melbourne was through the Internet. Ah! Well, I was still disappointed with the Melbourne Airport.

'Your passport, please.' The voice came from a man who looked like some airport official to me.

I lifted my head up and handed over my passport to him. He swiftly pulled out the declaration card tucked carefully between my passport pages and gave it a quick glance. Then he looked at me and further looked at the card. I wasn't sure at that point what was he judging.

I hated that look. I didn't know why, but it made me feel guilty.

'So you have some food items in your bag?'

'Yes, I do.'

This way, please. He signalled me to join one of the two queues which were moving towards the customs area. I collected my declaration card from him and joined the line he indicated.

I could see a lot of commotion at the end of what seemed like a long ant line. People were crawling centimetre by centimetre after every few minutes. I was getting restless. I couldn't even hobnob on my phone as it didn't have the local Aussie connection and I had not activated my roaming services.

After about what seemed like forever, it was my turn to face the custom officers. They asked me to put my big bag up. It passed through some kind of scanner and came out from the other side. There were two officers on each custom counter.

'Open your bag, please,' an officer instructed me in a firm tone.

'Do you have food items in it?'

'Yes, I do,' I said while opening up my bag.

The officer took charge of my bag as soon as I opened it and began rummaging it. Not that they had to dig deep. All the food items were kept right below the first layer of clothes. They took out all possible packets of food items from my bag and read labels on most of it.

'Did you pack your bag yourself?'

'Yes, I did, although—' They didn't let me finish my sentence.

'Do you know all the contents of this bag?'

'Yes, I do.'

'You know you are not allowed to carry these milk products and seeds into Australia. You can be fined for these things.'

After a small pause they spoke again. 'You can be fined for bringing these prohibited items to this country.'

Prohibited items? Since when had Kaju Barfi and Chikki become prohibited items in the world? For God's sake, these are food items and not bombs. I felt nothing short of a smuggler who was trying to bootleg some drugs or gold across the border. So much for my mom's enthusiasm for packing my bags, especially the food items! I could picture her face with the expression of fear and horror when I tell her about this food fiasco. It would be like telling a child that Santa is not real or that tooth fairy is an adult's way of fooling kids.

I felt extremely irritated towards my American cousins. After all, they had provided all the information about carrying food to my mother. Yes, I had decided in my mind that it was entirely their fault.

Somehow, I felt less guilty then.

'Be careful next time. You could be fined heavily,' the officer warned me before handing over my now much lighter bag. I didn't face any trouble in lifting it from there.

I pulled myself out of this initial shock and prodded ahead to clear the rest of the formalities, including calling up my parents. After some time, I hailed a cab and told the cabbie exactly where I wanted to go. I was impressed with the GPS features fitted into this cab and couldn't help but compare it to the autorickshaws in India. While my auto rides in India were almost always qualified in the category of verbal lashings, these cabs in Melbourne didn't require me to utter a single word except when I had to share my destination address. The cab driver was Indian, who perhaps guessed from my facial expressions that I was fresh out of the boat in this country. His friendly conversations amidst few bursts of laughter assuaged the initial shock which my mind had experienced since I first set foot in this country. I was overwhelmed by the friendly demeanour of the cabbie, who identified himself as Bunty, and he shared a lot of grapevine with me while his taxi galloped on the road.

I could see the speed signage on both sides of the roads, and as our cab was speeding towards 100 kilometres per hour, my heart was pulsating with equal vigour and excitement. Suddenly things didn't appear that bad. High-speed racing cars and glittering lights had in some way made me believe that my life was going to experience something exhilarating.

After a while, our cab came to a standstill at a traffic junction, and with that, I came back to the reality.

'Bunty, is it really very bad for Indians here? I mean, back in India, so much is written about the racial attacks on Indian, especially the students.' I mustered some courage to ask him this as this thought had been sitting on my mind ever since I learnt about my trip to Melbourne. Although I managed to pacify my parents when they raised their concern, I couldn't manage to rid my mind of the same worry, and so on this first instance when I met another Indian, I couldn't hold back my apprehensions.

'Don't worry! You will soon find out the reality,' Bunty replied but not before letting out a small giggle. I didn't know what to make out of his answer, and I didn't have the energy to probe him further. I just hoped in my heart that whatever he had said would be positive; after all, he had giggled before that.

I reached my destination with a letter from my college and thanked Bunty for his friendly gestures. It was a tall building with around twenty or thirty floors. I got down from the taxi and reached the main gate of the building with my heavy bags. Since there was practically no one in sight inside the building, I knocked lightly on the glass doors.

A man suddenly emerged out from behind the desk which read 'Concierge' on it in big silver colour.

'Another Indian,' I said to myself.

That man did something, and the entrance doors opened automatically. I was impressed.

I went inside with my bags and introduced myself.

'Hi, I am Sushant. I have just come from India.' And with that, I handed him a letter from my college.

He quickly scanned it and greeted me warmly.

'Hi, Sushant. Debbie had informed me about you. Welcome to Melbourne. I am Vijay, one of the concierge personnel for this building.'

I didn't know who Debbie was, but I was glad that Vijay was aware about my arrival and that I did not have to provide him any further explanations.

Vijay handed over me my bed number and keys to settle down. I felt a bit weird because instead of an apartment number, he gave me a bed number.

Nonetheless, I felt a bit relieved as I was tired from an entire day's journey across the hemispheres. My body needed some good dose of sleep while what my mind wanted was some peace to come out of the distress it felt at the sight of Melbourne's glitz and glamour.

'This way, please.'

I followed Vijay as he gestured towards the lift.

We entered into the lift as it arrived. Vijay pressed 26 on the level panel. I was pretty excited. I had never lived at such a high level in my life. We had a bungalow in India, so apartment living was completely new to me.

The lift stopped at level 26.

'This way, please.' Vijay again signalled to his right as he exited the lift.

'Sure.'

I just followed him mechanically.

As we entered the apartment, I was thrown further away from relief and peace as this apartment looked nothing like *my* room. It was more like a dormitory with nearly seven other beds apart from my bed. And if this was not enough, lo and behold, none of my roommates were what I had expected them to be in gender and in ethnicity. There was not even a single girl as my roommate, and of the seven people whom I was looking at, five were from Asian countries. I had begun to doubt myself by now and wondered if instead of a Melbourne flight I had boarded a flight to some Asian country. I was not being a racist, but come on! You too would be shocked if you went to a Chinese restaurant and the waiter served you a menu card for Middle Eastern cuisine. My dreams had not only shattered into tiny pieces, but I was scared that my heart could get an attack due to such unexpected turn of events since morning. If all the stories which I had heard from my NRI friends and relatives about life in developed countries were true, then so must be the case with the existence of ghosts, my popularity with girls, honesty of our politicians, and virginity of prostitutes.

Suddenly I was missing my own room at my home back in India, which was a big part of my life. I had my own room in my house, and my parents had given me all the liberty to reflect my soul and identity in it. I just loved my room, which I had created after days of shifting and reshifting furniture and arranging things till I found my perfect groove and everything looked just perfectly placed. I had spent several weekends enhancing its aesthetic value to match my taste and sensibilities.

A well-placed black leather beanbag was my favourite possession in the room, and I liked how it was positioned just close enough to the bookshelf to its right near the window. It was a space where I could be myself after the arduous hours of jostle with the outside world. I found a lot of solace in just sitting on my beanbag, strumming my guitar (which I barely knew how to play) or just reading books or even browsing on the Internet. A sense of loss had started to set deep within my heart.

I hadn't thought of my parents so kindly on this subject when I was in India. For me, it just appeared a part of their responsibility towards me. Perhaps I was beginning to think and feel different now.

I remembered how my life had always turned a different page when compared to others, and suddenly I had no complaints. I just sighed and looked back at my bed. Sleeping doesn't solve the problem, but neither does staying awake, so I went along with the first option and finally decided to give some rest to my mind and body. Silence of the cold white night just seeped into my heart and created a certain calmness which felt very unsettling at that moment. My mind was thronged with a potpourri of thoughts. I was a little jittery thinking about my new stint, a little excited about mingling with new people, a little bewildered about coping with the new culture, and amidst this entire rambling of thoughts, I don't quite remember when I slept off.

Next morning, I got up at the sound of my alarm clock and freshened up, beaming with enthusiasm for the induction programme. Then I realised it was only Saturday today and induction programme was scheduled for Monday morning at nine. The sun was cheerful after a long night, and I couldn't prevent my heart from yearning to go out into the streets of Melbourne City.

The mere thought of feeling warm sunrays on my skin made me feel joyous, so before the sun could change its mind, I pulled up a pair of black jeans and zipped up my jacket to go out and allowed the positivity of sunshine to cut through my cold and almost disappointing first experience of this country and this city.

The sunny day beckoned me to the city, and I was just getting drawn into walking around on the streets, just the way I used to do with my friends back in India. I hadn't made any friends here yet, so I did not feel like approaching anyone to accompany me. After a few moments of contemplating, I decided to venture out alone. As I stepped out of my building, I was welcomed by the gust of wind, which felt nothing short of a tight slap on my face. 'Ouch!' I murmured to myself and prodded ahead. Even though it was mid January, Melbourne was still cold, and the wind chill only made it tad bit more uncomfortable.

Technically, this part of the year was supposed to be warm and dry, but the grey skies were still dominating the city most of the time. I wondered if I should hire a taxi, but then I didn't have any particular place in mind to go, and neither did I have enough money in my pocket to splurge. I just wanted to walk aimlessly in the city and enjoy the mild sunshine.

A few metres ahead, there was a traffic signal, so I stopped, waiting for the walk signal to go green. I was told these signals normally turn green within a minute's wait, but today, it was still red even after a couple of minutes. I began to fidget with my jacket pocket and even had the urge to dodge the traffic and cross the road. At this point, I remembered the *easiness* of crossing roads in India and the numerous dodges which make one feel as though crossing road is a *kabaddi* game. Nevertheless, I pulled myself out of my thoughts and walked ahead.

As I entered the CBD area, a small smile broke out on my face. CBDs, or the central business districts, are one such part of the Australian cities which always buzzed with life and showed signs of human population, which is almost difficult to find on their otherwise mighty roads dominated with cars, trucks, and occasionally bikes. Spotting a two-wheeler was a rare event here, especially when I was just new to this country.

In Australia, red, purple, green, and pink colours are not only popular as favourite shades of hair colour, but these hues are also quite a sensation in the car segments. Before coming to Melbourne, the only place where I had seen these vibrant colours shine with pride was on girls' fingernails in the form of nail polish in our college back in India.

As if this amusement wasn't enough to awaken my senses, I also chanced upon men who had their nose pierced and adorned with nose pins and rings and who walked on roads with no sign of any awkwardness at all. They walked with aplomb, and there was practically no one else on the streets gaping at these men with frightened, confused, and shocked looks.

I had already witnessed too many revelations in too short a time, and my mind was buzzing with endless questions and curiosity.

Having walked a couple of kilometres by now, I wanted to sip on something really hot to thaw my body and regain my senses, so I entered into a coffee shop and ordered for a cup of cappuccino. While my order was being serviced, I noticed that most of the people in the coffee shop were having black coffee without sugar—the mere thought of which made me sick in the stomach. I definitely didn't want to feel this way right now, so I played safe and chose a coffee which was my usual order in India as well.

'One regular cappuccino,' shouted the girl from the counter. I picked up my coffee and some sugar sachets and found a sunny spot outside the shop to sit.

Hot coffee in mild sunshine and cold breeze was just what I needed at that point of time to feel comforted and normal, although I could have done just fine without the cold breeze.

The first sip of the hot cappuccino helped me to thaw my body and clear my mind. It took me into an introspection mode, a mode I was often used to getting into. I was a pretty chilled-out guy with an open mind, or so I liked to think about myself. Perhaps my shock value arose in Melbourne due to the real experience which I needed to test the openness of my thoughts.

'Excuse me! Are you from India?' A voice came from right behind my back.

I turned around to find a young girl about my age, dressed modestly in a pair of blue jeans and a white top. She had her hair tightly pulled back into a small ponytail, though I could tell from her look that her jet-black hair was silky and soft when treated more leniently.

'Yes, I am,' I replied while thinking all this.

The girl handed over a pamphlet to me with a faint smile. Before I could ask anything, she disappeared into thin air. I at once had the urge to throw away the pamphlet but couldn't find a bin around me. So I crushed it into a small clumsy ball and slipped it into my jacket's pocket. Just then, my phone rang. I looked at it and saw some unknown number calling. I didn't want to pick it up but, on second thought, answered the phone only to realise it was a customer care call from my phone service. They had called up to ask some routine questions.

In Australia, it's totally immaterial whether you make or receive a call—the first thing that you get to hear on the other side is either 'Hi! How are you doing today?' or 'Good, thanks, yourself?' And this is irrespective of the degrees of care you have or not have for each other. It appears quite welcoming when you make call for general inquiries, but if you are in hurry, then such rigmarole can sometimes get on to your nerves, especially for people like me.

College is that phase of a person's life when they get to explore the world, meet new people, and discover themselves.

In my case, I was unravelling the idiosyncrasies of a new country more than discovering myself. Australia was not only very much different from India, but it was also different from my perception of a glamorous, high-tech, and sophisticated developed country. I was preparing myself to withstand this shock, but what made my struggle harder was the Australian people's quirky way of talking. Not that I didn't understand English or couldn't speak it well, but what was I supposed to say when I was repeatedly being asked by strangers on roads, stores, and trains 'How you going?' Now what on earth did that seemingly harmless phrase even mean? Going by train, tram, or on foot, I was baffled by Aussies' eagerness and nosiness to know how I was going. Even worse was how they ever knew each time that I was going somewhere whenever I met one of their kinds. Was someone following me? Whoever had invented language as a means to facilitate communication between two individuals had clearly not lived in this part of the world. I was beginning to feel like a paranoid and had started to cringe at this question, just not knowing how to answer their intrusion in my personal matter.

Australians were a bunch of rude and nosy people who loved to meddle with other people's business. I had almost made up my mind about it. This trauma continued to haunt me until I was told by some kind soul 'How you going?' is an Aussie way of polite conversation of 'How are you?' It was another great example of how to complicate simple things in life, but I heaved a big sigh of relief when I finally understood this translation. At least I still had my privacy intact.

Anyway, after I hung up the phone, I realised that it had almost been four hours since I had left my apartment, and now I was beginning to feel a little hungry. There was another landmark which I had planned to see today ever since I had read about it on the Internet; it was the Salaam Namaste Bridge. It was the same bridge where Saif Ali Khan and Preity Zinta had danced and sung their way into their urban Aussie love story. I must confess at this point that after watching this movie in India, I had secretly nurtured a dream to come to Australia and soak myself in its beauty, glitz, and glamour.

Those were my dreams, and where I was right now was my reality. I decided to check out this bridge some other day after I had familiarised myself better with this city.

The rumbling sound from my stomach broke my chain of thoughts and indicated that my body needed some fuel now, so I decided to get some food. I grabbed an egg-and-spinach sandwich on my way back to my apartment and mulled over my decision about not approaching anyone from my room for my maiden city-seeing spree.

We all were new to this country, so perhaps I should take the initiative to break the ice and create a general sense of bonhomie with my roommates. By then, I had already started to miss my friends from India and the comfort of their presence in my life. After I reached back, I went to my room and smiled at the couple of guys who were there.

'How was your day?' one of the boys with distinct Mongolian features asked while smiling back at me.

'Yeah, it was good. I liked the sunshine although it was still very cold,' I replied, feeling amused over the power of a smile.

'Sorry, I didn't get your name. My name is Sushant Modi.'

'Hi, Shu-Shaat. I am Lee,' the Mongolian guy replied, almost butchering my name.

'No no, it is not Shu-Shaat.' I shook hands with him, feeling slightly irritated at my name being butchered. 'It's Su-Shaant.' I deliberately stretched the sound of *A* in my first name in my second attempt.

'Shu-Shaat . . . Shu-Shaat . . . Sorry, could you please spell that out for me?' Lee made another failed attempt at pronouncing my name.

'Sure. It's *S* as in *sugar*, *U* as in *umbrella*, *S* as in *sugar* again . . .' This saga continued first with my first name and then with my second name, and with each spell-out, I vividly remembered my nursery days.

'Sorry about that, Shu-Shaant,' Lee said, sounding a little embarrassed.

Well, at least Lee was able to pronounce my name. So what if it was a slightly different version of what my parents had intended it to be? In another five minutes, Lee and I exchanged some more pleasantries and got to know more about each other.

I had begun to thaw by then, although I am not sure if it was because I had finally made a friend or because the temperature inside our room was warmer than the outside. It's amazing how the warmth of a companionship can cut through even the harshest coldness of the loneliness.

Monday morning, I got up with a new enthusiasm and hope for life. I was told that all students under our exchange programme would be inducted together for the new semester. I wore my favourite blue jeans with a gunshot and teamed it up an algae-green shirt. I looked at myself in the mirror and felt quite pleased with my look. An almost-faint smile broke out on my face. I remembered how my mom would get displeased when I wore these gunshot jeans, which she clearly considered torn and tattered—something which a child of highly reputed professors shouldn't wear.

I brushed aside her thoughts with a sense of freedom and quickly looked at my watch. I was ready much before the time and just didn't know what to do next. I checked on Lee to see if he needed me for something, but he too was doing well.

Suddenly I heard an almost scream-like announcement in the corridor outside our room.

'Who has dumped that stinky tissue roll in the bin?' shouted a rather tall boy who had a disgruntled look on his face.

'For those who do not know, please flush the tissue roll back in the toilet after you have cleaned your bum. The toilet is stinking badly right now,' the tall boy said, appearing as though he would puke right away.

'Yuck! Now who on earth would dump the dirty tissues in the dustbin?' I murmured while looking at Lee.

'I know who has done this,' Lee whispered to me.

'Who?' I quizzed Lee.

'You see that guy in blue T-shirt and black shorts? He's the one who did that,' Lee said this while pointing to a guy standing several feet away from us. He was a short guy with curly hair and a pale complexion. The look on his face was that of confusion and fear. I pitied him and thanked God that I was aware of how to use the tissue rolls in the toilet—most importantly after it has fulfilled its purpose. The crowd dispersed quickly after a bit of discussion and giggles, and so did Lee and I.

I was feeling upbeat about meeting new people and making new friends, so I headed towards my class after wandering around for a while and feeling recharged by the warmth of the morning. There was still a good fifteen minutes before the start of the induction programme, so I thought of buying a newspaper in the meantime.

This idea was primarily driven by my addiction for reading paper in the morning, and secondarily, I thought I could pick up some topics of discussions while making new friends, along with getting to know more about this country. My earlier experiences clearly weren't helping me here. So I headed towards the nearest convenience store to pick up a newspaper. Unlike India, here I wasn't sure which newspaper was the best, so I quickly scanned the store to see whether I find any trace of newspapers or not, and to my good luck, I spotted a stand where a few newspapers were stacked.

'I'll get a copy of this one,' I told the woman behind the counter after picking up a copy of *The Age* newspaper.

'Sure. Dollar twenty, please. Thank you,' she said without looking at me. She was a rather cute-looking Caucasian girl, perhaps in her late teens, with freckled cheeks and skin so smooth that I was almost tempted to feel it. She did not fall into the typical category of 'beautiful', but she still had something very intriguing about her smile which made my eyes glue to her. What I had before my eyes was making me feel my heartbeat.

'Dollar twenty, please,' she repeated herself, albeit this time looking at me, which made me realise that I was indeed gaping at her. I felt embarrassed, almost like the time when I was a kid and I used to get caught by my mother removing candies from the jar, which she would keep on the top shelf of the kitchen cabinet. I sheepishly looked aside and focused on what she had just blurted out.

Twenty dollars for a newspaper? That's ridiculous. What has the world come to? I thought to myself. The idea of reading news suddenly didn't appear so alluring to me. I quickly multiplied twenty by fifty and realised that a thousand rupees was categorically way too much for a newspaper by any standards. In India, I could buy newspapers for more than a year in thousand rupees as against one newspaper in Australia. Even if I ignored the exchange rate between INR and AUD, the cost of the paper still didn't match the denominations in India. I mustered some guts and told the girl that I had only five dollars with me so I will buy the paper sometime later.

For some reason, she appeared very flummoxed. I wasn't sure if it was my accent which was confusing her or if that was the general look on her face. Those puffy eyelids and thin slit-like eyes made her expressions absolutely inscrutable. Anyway, I tried once again. I pushed the paper towards her over the counter and told her that I don't have twenty dollars to pay for this paper.

'Oh, no, no, no! This is not for twenty dollars. This is for dollar twenty,' she told me, but I still had no change of expression on my face. She then pointed out at the corner of the paper and told me, 'Dollar twenty.'

I looked at the newspaper corner where she was pointing to, and my jaw dropped down in complete shock. It read '$1.20'.

'Oh! Okay.' I smiled at her while my face had turned crimson, or at least I felt so because I could feel the heat generated rushing towards my cheeks and ears. I could suddenly empathise with the guy from my apartment who had dumped his faecal tissue in the bin! I felt sorry for him as I did for myself. I immediately paid for the paper and disappeared from there at a speed which was greater than my personal best in my sporting career. Now, how could I have known that dollar twenty was indicative of one dollar and twenty cents? Couldn't these people say something as it actually meant? I tried to justify my thought process to myself.

I felt embarrassed and a bit edgy too, and by then, all my excitement for the induction programme had just vanished away. Anyway, despite my wobbly mind, I sat through the programme and tried to absorb as much information as I could without letting my mind wander into the morning incident and dwell over my perplexity around dollars and cents.

There were around one hundred and twenty six people in my batch, of which seventy were Asians, twenty were Indians, and the rest thirty-odd were a mix of Australians, Europeans, Africans, and Americans. Yes, I had experienced yet another eye-opener with the revelations that Indians were not considered Asians. The word *Asian* was typically used for those who came from China, Korea, Japan, or any one of the South East Asian countries, like Malaysia, Thailand, Indonesia, Vietnam, etc. *What a waste of learning geography in the school*, I thought to myself. Meanwhile, everybody was provided with an opportunity to stand up and introduce themselves to the class, along with a line on what made them choose this course. I could hardly understand a dozen students' names, leave alone remembering them. Some of the names didn't even sound like names.

Choosing a right name is certainly an art, and this sensibility dawned upon me when I heard some really quirky names which sounded like a spoon falling on the ground or a bottle being opened up or a child puking. I haven't mentioned these names here primarily because I do not want to hurt anyone's sentiments and, secondarily, because I do not know how to spell out these names. This situation reminded me of the famous song from *Delhi Belly* movie 'Bhag bhag DK Bose DK Bose DK', which was more of an insinuation than a suggestion to all the DK Boses in our country.

Little did I know then that my one year of stay in Australia would see me befriend several people named Lee, Kris, Nick, Mandy, Cathy, and others, most of which were shortened for Krishnamurthy, Nicholas, Mandeep, and Katherine in reality. After my initial difficulty in comprehending these abridged names, I finally agreed with Shakespeare and his million-dollar question 'What's in the name?'

Even though short and sweet names are most preferred by people, their meanings should not be ignored, or else you may end up been called Rick Shaw, Hugh Jass, Dan Druff, or Dick Hyman, all of which are real names of real people in Australia.

Chapter 3

It's the Aussie Way

Next few days were easy as there was no drama. I had not made any attempt to go anywhere outside, apart from my routine trips to my apartment and university and then came the proverbial weekend. I was supercharged for this one as I had lots of whims and fancies around weekends Down Under, which I wanted to experience. I wanted to explore my concept of freedom here by unwinding and have some fun to undo the damage which this country had done to my belief system.

I had made a few friends in the university, so I thought I would plan something fun with them and explore the city only to realise that everyone already had some agendas chalked up on their minds, most of which were important. Doing laundry, cleaning the room, and finishing a project in Network Technology Integration topped my list as well after my discussion with them. As the weekend approached its end, I felt utter disbelief, thinking about how I had actually spent the glorious Saturday and Sunday against what perception I originally had in my mind.

I never knew my idea of fun and unwinding would translate into washing, cleaning, and finishing up projects over the weekend. I was in a developed country for an exchange programme, and this is what I was doing. What stories would I share my friends when I go back to India? Amidst everything else, this thought weighed heaviest on my mind.

I had thought developed countries were supposed to have more luxury and more convenience built into their lifestyle, but little did I know I had to play the roles of *Ramesh dhobi*, *Shanta bai*, and *Ramu kaka* all rolled into one in order to enjoy the loftiness in my folk's imaginations back in India. Never before had I felt the word *developed* being abused so much, and all these years, I thought only Indians were the hard-working people.

Time flew by, but I had not completely recovered from these blows. Our term break was just around the corner, and I had once again started daydreaming about all the fun I could now then have in Melbourne with my newly made friends. But just like the mundane hollow promises made by our politicians before elections every year, my dreams too went kaput when I was advised by my new friends to take up some part-time job in order to earn some extra bucks for my occasional indulgence and most often for the survival itself. So I got thinking over what part-time job I could do. I mean, I had never 'worked' before in my life, nor did I have the thoughts about jobs and companies anywhere on my radar yet. I was just a sophomore, and I still had to build a memory bank for my lifetime, memories which would linger in our minds for the rest of our lives. Sigh!

There were plenty of places which needed helping hands in their tasks, so I thought I could pick up what suits me the best in the area of my interest—computer and technology.

In the coming week, I received rejections from fifteen different places that I had applied to as a part-time employee, while most of my friends had already found some takers. Every rejection application stated that I was too inexperienced, and I also didn't have suitable qualification to be an intern with them. Not only was my confidence bulldozed completely, but my skills were also being looked at dubiously.

I was not completely sure if it was my rejection from the employers or the fact that I was the only one in my group who hadn't secured a job yet which played heavily on my mind after being honoured with fifteen rejection letters.

'I can't be that bad! Or could I be? After all, I was chosen from my entire batch for this exchange programme. There had to be something good about me—something which would make someone pay me some money.' I was full of self-doubts at that point of time and felt worthless amongst my friends.

The thought of my Indian friends spending endless hours in the college canteen, going for movies stealthily, and guzzling vodka flashed before my eyes constantly. If it wasn't for this stupid exchange programme, I too would be busy creating some memories with my friends.

Suddenly I felt very angry at our princi who had, in the first place, suggested my name for this exchange programme.

It was then that I decided to follow the herd and do what my other friends had opted for—dishwashing in restaurants, working as security, doing sales job, working as a checkout operator in superstores, cleaning in apartments and hotels, taking orders at fast-food joints, as well as taking calls at the call centres.

The fact that I had never performed any of these tasks before was not so much unnerving as the idea of my folks knowing about my association with these. What would they think if they knew I was scrubbing or cleaning in Australia? I could picture a look of disappointment on their faces.

I was not particularly great at talking, so I struggled to get even these jobs.

I was caught in a vicious circle of work dilemma in Australia. I was not getting a job because I did not have 'local experience', and I could not have local experience as I did not have any job—only if I could make my prospective employers understand this. I didn't know which one of these was an actual problem for me. It had almost been two weeks since I had started applying for some part-time jobs, but the lady luck had refrained from smiling upon me.

Although there was no pressure on me to work, I didn't know what to do with my extra time, especially when everyone in my batch was working hard and earning some extra bucks, including Lee.

My daily job search routine would involve sipping on my cup of hot chocolate while checking my emails, job portals, and networking websites. Of course, I was doing all this to find a job for myself; otherwise, I wouldn't have wasted my precious online time on such a thing. I had great computer skills and knowledge, so I was quite optimistic about landing a job within a few days, but at that time, I didn't know about the turnaround time of application process in Australia. The first job profile which I had applied for had published revert time of four weeks (from the application closing date), which had almost thrown me out of my senses. I, anyway, didn't get through it. This was my first job application, and that number had reached seventeen by now. Most of my applications got rejected with any of these typical opening lines:

1. After careful consideration, we regret to advise that we will not be progressing with your application for this role.
2. We have reviewed your résumé, and while it is of a high standard, unfortunately, at this time your application has been unsuccessful.

3. After reviewing your details, we have decided not to progress with your candidature for the role as we have received interest from candidates with experience more closely matching our client's requirements.

The versatile, talented, and valued computer guru from India was now full of self-doubts in Australia. My confidence had started to plummet exponentially, and I had begun to wonder if I was really unequipped to fit in the workforce here. Everyone around me tried to pacify me by doling out words like 'It's just a matter of time', 'Don't worry you'll get something better', 'Be patient', and whatnot. With each phrase, I felt like shutting down my ears. I had not shared with Lee, Nick, and few of my other friends that I had become so desperate to get a job that I had started applying for positions which did not have the remotest connection to my interest, skills, or qualifications. I was not particularly proud of these vacancies. I was somebody in my college in India, and now I was grappling to get selected for a part-time job as well. I had become nobody now. Apart from everything else which was associated with getting a job, my identity was the most important and non-negotiable factor for me. But I felt I was losing my grip on that now.

Time flew, and some more days went by, but I was still a jobless guy from overseas. After coming to Australia and some tête-à-tête with my friends, I had realised that getting a job would not be very easy, but what I had not realised was that it would be this hard. It appeared like a mirage to me. With each application, I would raise my hopes of getting employed, but gradually that hope would disappear into oblivion too.

Eventually, the sympathy words around me turned into advice box with nobody to everybody suggesting something useful to me.

'Apply for a part-time job at XYZ. It will add value to your experience.'

'You love computers. Why don't you try something in JB Hi-Fi?' JB Hi-Fi is a popular electronics store which sells everything from computers, cameras, laptops, DVDs, and other smart items for this smart generation.

I hoped that one day unsolicited advice and suggestions would start getting charged. The more you give, the more you pay. Time flew again, and two more weeks passed by now.

'*Sushi*, are you ready? I'll get late for my work,' Lee yelled from the alley of our building while trying to wear his shoes at the same time. This is what Lee used to call me with affection.

'Yes, I am ready.' I said this while ensuring my hair looked tidy. I rushed out of the room towards the alley. Before that, I did a final mirror check on my look in the dressing mirror and straightened my shirt collar.

'Is my trousers crumpled?' I asked Lee while looking into my wallet for the myki card.

A myki card is smart travel card which can be used for travel in public transports like trams, trains, and buses in Melbourne. I was totally in awe of this system, which seemed so much hassle-free and freed us from queuing up for daily purchase of tickets—although I always thought that Melbourne had costly public transportation system, and hence, I was very judicious in using my myki card. Perhaps my Gujju genes weren't as dormant after all.

'You look just fine,' Lee answered while looking at my uniform of black shirt and black trousers and smiled at me. Within twenty minutes, I reached my new workplace. I got down from the tram, wore my black sweater and ID card, and entered a classy Italian restaurant. My shift was about to begin in fifteen minutes. I hoped to find myself a job which did justice to my education, work experience, and self-esteem. Till then, I preferred choosing a something over nothing.

Finally, what had landed in my fate was the vacancy for a dishwasher in the Italian restaurant on a street just three blocks away from my uni. The sight of dirty and soiled utensils was not perky, and neither were the painfully long hours of scrubbing cosy or plush in any aspect. I was living the perfect dream of studying in a foreign country—that's what my friends in India perhaps might be thinking. The only difference was that my dreams were slowly turning into nightmares. Fully advanced classrooms missed advanced students—by all means, I was the brightest student who did not get befuddled when a professor wrote 2 divide by 4 equals 0.5. I mean, really? Cute girls in short skirts missed cuteness, cosy beds missed cosiness in harsh winters, and rocking weekends became scrubbing and cleaning weekends.

A few months ago, I had left my home for a study tour to Melbourne, and within these few months, I had learnt much more about life than I had ever wanted to. I was in a foreign place all by myself, but I had made good friends, and I was also looking after myself well. I certainly missed my life back in India, and to be uprooted from a place and people that you love is not something that you strive for. But I was proud of how my head and heart were guiding me through all these.

By now, I had also decoded Bunty's (my first cabbie) parting dialogue which had left me wondering about my fate. I soon realised that the hype surrounded racial attacks on Indian students wasn't as grim as it was being portrayed by the Indian media back in India. There were a few attacks and deaths in the Indian community, but these weren't happening because Indian students were racially attacked. There were a lot of reasons and justifications about the real situations, but apart from all these eccentricities, what gave me peace of mind and comfort to my parents' hearts was that I was safe here. Nothing else mattered to them as much at this point of time in their lives.

Thanks to my wonderful habit of reading newspaper daily, it didn't take me long enough to realise that just like in India, everything makes news in Australia too, and I mean literally everything. From the moment we woke up in the morning to the time we roll under our blankets in the night, each moment of our day is blasted with overdose of news. Right from the infamous, dramatic events of Hollywood stars to the twisted tales of politics and countless cases of corruption, news pieces keep fluctuating on our mental graphs. At times, their volatility strikes our day with thoughts and contemplation, and other times, they crash our minds with the sheer absence of their relevance in anyone's life.

Multimedia has further heightened the extent to which news can penetrate into our lives. Even if you wish to leave your newspapers aside for a day, how will you escape the TV channels, social networking websites, and smartphones, which won't let your mind rest in peace? Our lives are already traumatised with dedicated news channels which present every miniscule thing like a 'never before seen' event, not to forget the theatrical impact which is accorded to all the news items for creating the thrills and frills of daily soaps. I mean, who cares if LiLo (Lindsay Lohan) has been caught doped (again!) or how low Delta Goodrem's neckline plunges each year in her appearance as judge on *The Voice* show? Don't we see enough of such acts on televisions and in movies that now we have to read about these as well?

And why should we poke our noses into the receding hairline, diminishing waistline, and sucked-in cheeks of Shane Warne? We all know that he was smitten by his former lady love who was not so long ago known as the bold and beautiful

Indian *bahu*, Liz Hurley. Weren't we already sniffing too much into the lives of such people by prying on their health and might-sink career that the media is further attempting to bring alive their daily woes to public?

With the burgeoning of social networking websites, a new genre of users has burgeoned—that of wannabe journalists. Every person tries to propagate, rather report, news in the most uncouth manner, killing the very spirit of journalism. Forget the gravitas of the language chosen—most of these people don't even verify the veracity of the information they come across before posting it for others to read. Things get worse when such rumours come accompanied with the individual's stinking thoughts laced with hinted expletives. We all like to be aware of things happening inside and outside our country, but when any random information occupies the slot in breaking news ticker to an extent of becoming a trend, our minds automatically get switched off.

Whether or not Ms Gillard's partner is gay and why Tony Abbott never ceases to commits faux pas or if shows like *Celebrity Splash* represent a decline of intellectual TV viewers in Australia and are merely pieces of information which do not require to be tweeted, retweeted, posted, scrapped about, or flashed in the top headlines and breaking news section of any form of media or multimedia. We can, of course, choose to laugh about such news or turn deaf ears to them, but wouldn't it be better if the media stopped perceiving every incident as sensational or scandalous and focused on issues which were relevant to us? So when I felt the need (and when I could manage to squeeze in some time from my busy studies) for relevant news to be entertaining or amusing, I tuned into my TV flavour Al Jazeera, Discovery, or BBC.

One remarkable thing which I discovered quite early during my stay in Australia was the queue formation. Whether you are in the shopping malls, ticket counters, train stations, grocery stores, petrol stations, or any other place, people here have the innate tendency to form queues and stand. Now it's a different matter back in India—at least two to three more people could have found their way into the queue between each one-hand distance as leaving any *extra* space is considered a waste of space by most. I remember how we would shove one another and jostle like a bunch of bees, whether it was at our canteen counter or bus stops or even at the ticket counters in multiplexes. After all, we come from a place where people stand so close to one another that their closeness facilitates easy transfer of smell from their armpits. Fortunately, the good old rule of 'Stand at one-hand distance' from our school days is the unsaid rule Down Under, and thank God for that.

During my initial days in Melbourne, there were lots of getting-to-know introduction kind of meetings, dinners, and students' get-together which I had to attend.

In one such catch-up, a friend of my batchmate was casually chatting with me, asking about how I liked being here, whether I was enjoying the weather, and other questions which normally fit such formats of short talks. She told me that since I was new to Melbourne, my weekends must generally be flat out like a lizard drinking. I don't recollect what happened in the next fifteen to twenty seconds as I went blank after that statement.

All my life, I had never heard of lizard drinking, forget it being in a flat state. My mind just stopped processing information, and my ears refused to hear anything more. I wondered what she meant by that phrase. Was I supposed to say yes or no, or give a more elaborate answer to it? I didn't want to feel stupid but the truth is I felt like one. So I did what our minds are best trained to do in such situations—nod my head. I nodded in affirmation, looking at that friend, who then happily jumped on to another topic, and I sighed with relief.

It was later that I understood the hidden meaning behind lizard drinking and its flat-out condition. Let's say if I had to use that phrase, I would have just said, 'Your weekends must be *extremely busy.*' Yes, *extremely busy* is what that seemingly meaningless slang meant, which had almost managed to throw me out of my wits.

The laid-back approach of Aussies is not only reflected in their lifestyle, but it also resonates in their language. They just love to shorten words and add an *O* after it, like *ambo, brolly, rego, garbo, aggro,* and *arvo,* which otherwise mean *ambulance, umbrella, registration, garbage, aggressive, afternoon.* Phew! So much for the love of English language.

I too got affected under this 'let's shorten everything' policy, adhered to it with utmost sincerity in Australia, and so my name got squeezed and cramped into Sushi, from the much-loved version of Sushant! What could I do? I was just trying to feel the Aussie love each time someone addressed me with my newly earned name. And when nothing else made sense to me, I just threw the most-loved phrase of Aussies: 'No worries.' Just like abracadabra, this phrase could magically mellow down any hostile conversation or even make the other person feel thanked for.

Nevertheless, there were a few other things here which I just couldn't understand during my warming days—like the 5 p.m. curfew rule. I mean, even my college hostels in India were more liberal in kicking off the curfew at nine thirty in the night. Sigh!

There was so much we wanted to do after finishing our classes, completing the assignments, and preparing for the next day but so little could actually be achieved in Australia during the curfew hours. Couple of months in Melbourne has empowered me to train my mind to stop thinking about a much happening life and desiring for a freshly brewed coffee after five o'clock in the evening, leave alone experiencing the vibrancy and enigma of late night pubs and restaurants, which had enticed me ever since I had looked up Melbourne on the Internet.

What had initially started as an irritation had slowly transformed into my frustration and later into resignation and cynicism toward this system. After all, what could a simple Indian boy like me do to shake this system? The image of a neon-lit city hustling and bustling during the late hours of the night mocked at me with its guts out. The entire city slept after 5 p.m. on weekdays, and on weekends, only a few places stayed open till late night, forcing me to reminisce on the idea of nightlife from a Hollywood movie.

When I closed my eyes, I could see the flashes of well-lit skyscrapers, long roads full of fancy cars, tidy pavements, well-dressed men and women walking arms in arms, laughing talking and coming in and out of restaurants, clubs, malls, and stores, creating a perfect scene for a great evening in Melbourne. When I opened my eyes, I could see the reality.

Month 2

Chapter 4

Innateness, aka Indianness

It had been two months since I had arrived in Australia when one morning Lee took me out with him to visit one of his friends.

'Come on, Sushi, you will enjoy meeting him. He is Indian too.' Lee had insisted that since his friend was Indian, I might find some useful tips for my survival here.

'Yeah, okay, although I don't know why being an Indian is an advantage. You are not Indian. We still get along very well.'

'You know I didn't mean that.'

I knew what he meant, and in the absence of anything interesting to do, I agreed to go along with him.

Meeting Kris turned out to be very interesting for me because apart from his usual quirkiness, he had also got me thinking about our Indian fascinations with certain commodities which are an integral part of our life like, Parachute coconut oil, Cycle brand *agarbattis*, Maggi Masala noodles, Red Label tea, Amul butter, 50-50 biscuits, and pirated Hindi movie DVDs. These fascinations do not end in India; rather, we transcend the political and geographical barriers and bring these fascinations along with us to the land of opportunities ruled by Obama, the Queen, Gillard, and others of their ilk.

We just can't live without our bimonthly visit to Patel's shop for our daily dose of Indianness. By saying *we*, I do not mean only those who leave India for a short term on business visas or work permits to fulfil their dreams of earning dollars, pounds, euros, yen, and other forms of currency and live the big Indian dream of going to a 'phoren' country but also those globetrotters who have either become NRIs or bequeathed their Indian citizenships completely. I was seeing it in Kris, and I had seen it amongst my NRI cousins and few other NRI friends too who would occasionally visit India during their holidays.

'So what are you studying here?' Kris asked me nonchalantly.

'Oh! I am studying network engineering, and I came here two months ago.' I added that extra bit of unsolicited information to avoid being asked any further question from Kris. Clearly, I didn't know him well.

'Sounds good! So how are you liking it so far?' Kris popped up another question, taking me completely by surprise. I may have been biased about him because of his first impression on me, which led me to perceive him in a different light. However, after meeting him several times in the coming days, the invisible wall of awkwardness between Kris and me gradually disappeared, and I began to see the person beyond his dozen peculiarities.

At five feet eight inches tall, Kris stood slightly under my ears, but his olive complexion and charming talks made him close to me very soon. He was a peculiar guy, and I had never met anyone like him before. Those who didn't know him well might not agree with me. He was a friend's friend, but at the same time, he had a streak of fierce competitive spirit in his character. He liked to stay ahead of his peers and was absolutely anal about his health and well-being.

He would pop up a pill at the drop of a hat. He literally ran a pharmacy store in his room. He had a box filled up with tablets of all colours, shapes, and sizes, ranging from diarrhoea to constipation, headaches to painkillers, cold to fever, and anything and everything defined in between these symptoms. His general health was far from ailments, but he liked to swallow a pill or run to a pharmacist whenever he faced a situation which his medically intuitive mind and his box of tablets could not solve.

Lee was right when he mentioned to me that I might find some survival tips from Kris. Although I wouldn't call Kris stingy, he was great with his money and kept a close tab on every cent that he spent. Kris also loved talking about investments and how to spend money in the most judicious manner. I learnt quite a lot being in his company, some of which still come handy to me till this date.

Kris also enjoyed lots of female attention with his good looks, great academic performance, and friendly attitude, but he still couldn't find a girlfriend. This concern occupied the top position in his list of worries and fears when he had nothing more to worry on his medical or health front.

His friendly attitude surely made him approachable, but he wasn't as charming to talk when it came to girls. Let's say in some way or the other, he lacked the gift of gab. He would often start up on a good note with girls; however, he would also often wind up saying something awkward while talking to them, and hence, his relationships and flings had never culminated into anything serious.

Despite the similarity in our nationality and our culture and the fact that Kris and I gelled well, I had a deeper connection with Lee. There was something real between Lee and me that bonded us so well. I can certainly say he had quickly become one of my good friends. His carefree attitude and jovial demeanour never allowed a dull moment to exist between us, especially when we were together, and I often wondered how perfect his life is. In my heart, I used to envy him at times.

Lee was six feet one inch tall and clearly overlooked my shoulder. His slender body often reminded me of snake, especially when I first saw him dance at a nightclub on one weekend. He had learnt a few dance forms and loved to groove unabashedly whenever his favourite music played in the club. Lee was different from other Chinese boys whom I had met at my uni. He wasn't particularly a scholar of our class, but he was doing pretty well. He would often tell me that life is too short and we must live it to the fullest. He knew so many things that at times I felt like a complete daft in front of him. He could jive. He could play the keyboard. He enjoyed snowboarding. He was learning calligraphy. And best of all, he had already stepped out into the big bad world and gathered work experience of four years before he joined this course in Melbourne University.

Not that I ever competed with him, but I think unconsciously or perhaps sometime consciously, I aspired to be like him. I had high regard for him and thoroughly enjoyed his company.

Although he was my good friend and we had shared quite a few laughter and great moments in our lives in Melbourne, he had never shared much about his family with me. Any attempt from my end would get thwarted by him, which sometimes made me feel that he was quite shallow at the emotional front until the day I came across a very bitter truth about his life.

Month 3

Chapter 5

T for *Technology*

'What is it? Some new Hollywood movie?' Cathy, one of my friends at the uni, asked me with complete ignorance. She thought Earth Hour was just another movie like *Rush Hour*, *127 Hours*, and *The Darkest Hour*, and with this question, I ascertained that she clearly was not active on any form of networking websites or even using the Internet, leave alone reading newspapers.

I explained to her about the 'one-hour no electricity' campaign across the globe and how it would help us save our Earth. Apart from the still-existing ignorance about this campaign amongst people, what startled me further was their reluctance to participate in it. I wondered how difficult it was for people to sacrifice electricity for just one hour. Could they not just sleep during that time and get done with it?

Determined to participate in it, I convinced Lee and Kris to contribute as well, so three of us decided to spend that evening together at Kris's house. Moreover, since Earth Hour this year was on a Saturday, Lee and Kris readily agreed to sacrifice their one hour of electricity foreplay. After we reached Kris's house, we switched off entire lights of the house at 8.30

p.m. sharp and lit just a couple of candles to allow us to at least see one another.

For a moment, it felt like a scene straight out of some Bollywood movie, but in another moment, this feeling died down in the lack of any background music. Anyway, after doing my bit of lighting up Kris's house, we came and sat down on the couch.

'Let's have a beer. I have already chilled them in the fridge before you guys came,' Kris said.

'Sounds like a plan to me.' Lee jumped at the idea of having a beer, so I asked them to go ahead, with a promise that I will join them soon. I had decided to have beer only after we had successfully participated and completed the Earth Hour.

Kris and Lee soon popped open two bottles of beer and stepped out into the backyard.

'Sushant, come, let's cheers together,' Kris shouted.

'But I am not drinking yet.'

'I know, but at least join us in raising a toast to our effort.'

I liked his idea, so I joined them outside in the backyard. Although we had switched off all the lights, it was still pleasantly lit up in the moonlight. All three of us raised a toast to this exciting plan and our fun hour ahead.

After a success toasting and some laughter, I got back into the house while Kris and Lee got on with their conversations. I must admit that the clinking of the beer bottles and the sprinkle of few drops around was tempting enough for me to join the boys, but I held back.

I picked up the remote to watch TV but then remembered about my pledge, so I quietly kept it down. I looked around to see what I could do next, and I saw Kris and Lee staring at me with looks which clearly conveyed that they didn't think too highly of my idea. I immediately picked up a magazine to read to avoid their eye contact, but after about five minutes of wrinkled eyelids and straining eyes, I gave up. I mean, although I was used to reading books under my tiny reading light inside my blanket at home, candlelight reading was a bit of pain, so I slid my magazine under the cushion and picked up my laptop for browsing the Internet. It's amazing how the Internet had opened up completely different worlds of fun, information, and amusements to cater to various senses of human beings. I could hear voices of Kris and Lee chatting in the backyard and laughing. I was quite certain that they were laughing at my predicament; nonetheless, I was glad at least they were having a good time.

Alas! We had switched off the modem's power too, so there was no Internet connectivity to the laptop. A fully charged laptop appeared completely useless to me at that moment. I was beginning to get a little irritated and badly wanted to ridicule this idea of Earth Hour celebration had it not been my suggestion.

'Damn you, Earth Hour!' I let out my exasperation in a low voice, lest my other two friends thought I wasn't enjoying it myself.

I was wondering what I could do next and realised that I really had no work. Dinner was over, lights were off, TV and magazines were out of question, and the Internet was elusive. I mean, I had good one hour with me with absolutely no agenda, and still, I couldn't remember a single activity which I could do in this hour. I had dug my own grave. Switching off electricity was actually pushing me towards boredom. I was beginning to feel restless now, so I got up and thought of taking a stroll in the backyard, but the tick-tock of the clock was weighing too heavy on me, plus I would have to tell Kris and Lee that I actually didn't know what to do without electricity. I couldn't even talk to anyone on the phone as it was low on battery and I didn't want it to get switched off in this dark hour.

I loitered around for a while and then came back to my good old couch. After making myself comfortable on it, I actually began to wonder how electricity had crept into our lives and transformed from a human discovery to a human necessity. Our days start with switching on the lights and end with switching it off, with all the hours in between filled with myriad moments of indulgence and dependence on electricity.

Most of us couldn't imagine our days without cell phones, laptops, iPods, TVs, microwaves, washing machines, refrigerators, dishwashers, and several other gadgets, leave aside smaller tools like an iron, hairdryer, electric shaver, blender, globe, and in my case, a fan too! Yes, believe it or not, I just cannot sleep without running a fan even in the thickest of Melbourne winter. From thinking how easy it would be to sleep during Earth Hour and not feel a pinch of it, my mind was just staring at the motionless fan. Sigh! Moving on, imagine the horror of starting your mornings without your daily dose of caffeine. Ouch! I know it hurts.

For most of us, our worlds would come crashing down with a serious lack of fuel, but when have, we learnt to be proactive. This has been the first time in my life when I have actually realised how much we, as a human race, abuse electricity. In India too, I used to participate in Earth Hour, but then it had not affected my life in a manner as it has this time in Australia.

Despite enjoying all the luxuries, Indians still have alternatives for carrying out their daily chores sans electricity. Be it washing clothes, cleaning utensils, sweeping, mopping, cooking, or even plain communication and entertainment—everything could be performed to perfection without thunder and bolts. Nevertheless, one hour of no electricity had certainly sabotaged an hour of my life, and so I had decided to become more aware of my daily electricity quotient and help save our Earth.

I couldn't wait to share my enlightenment with Kris and Lee and with every other person I could think of in my life. It was a eureka moment for me. We need to get into the court and play our games before all our machines and gadgets gulp down Earth for their electricity appetite. I had sort of learnt my big lesson in electricity in a developed nation and decided to take it back with me when I go back to India. For now, I did not want to resist the aroma and call of Hoegaarden, so I went out into the backyard, where Lee and Kris were cheering up life, and I joined them too. The first sip of Hoegaarden had almost instantaneously assuaged the pain of no electricity in the last one hour of my life and further faded its memory with each sip that flowed down my throat.

After this incident, I often pondered over how different our worlds would become without the daily click, swipe, buzz, and screech of inventions and modern technology existing in our lives. Sounds which were earlier considered noise had now become forerunner of our progress and comfort. Over time, technology has created a certain sense of freedom in our life where we are no longer bound to sit at home to take or make calls, where we are not required to carry a wallet full of notes and coins to shop, and where we are not forced to flip through the pages of big books in huge libraries to gather information about anything living or dead.

The degree by which technology had increased comfort and convenience in our lives was not more than the degree by which it was also exposing, sharing, and leaking our personal data to the outside world. From food and drinks to clothes and shoes and toothpastes and shampoos, every single product and our choice of its brand gets registered with the debit/credit card companies. We flash our cards, swipe it on the machine, and come back home with a smile on our faces without realising that we were creating trails for all these big companies to take a peek into our lives and monitor each and every thing that we enjoy.

Maybe not in entirety, but at least to some extent we are treading towards the dilemma and complexities of Truman, whose life was being monitored 24/7 by someone who claimed to have accorded a comfortable life to him.

I have also wondered in the past how our Gmail inbox or Facebook wall showed advertisements which were based on our recent search history or browsing pattern on the Internet. Modern-day technology allows not only our computers to remember our online activities, but it also gives a sneak peek of it to the giants who dominate the online world. Right from our mobile phones to the Internet connections and plastic money, every avenue of technology allows someone to track our habits. We don't waste even a single second in scrolling down to the bottom of any web page before clicking on I Agree, but we take hours in wondering about how we got such nasty spam emails in our mailbox.

Most of the companies share their customer data like emails and phone numbers with their allied vendors, who eventually target us and our privacy. Information like birthdate, email address, phone number, residential info, and family members' names is not difficult to gather in this viral age. Frauds and hackers benefit most from such situations—they take no time in draining our bank balances, transferring our phone numbers, and many a times, even shopping online.

Is there a solution for such menace? Maybe there is, maybe there is not. All I wanted to do then was to thank God that our dishwashers, refrigerators, and microwaves were still just plain machines and equipment which are determined to make our lives easier without having any extra pair of eyes for spying on us to say, '*Bigg Boss khush hue.*'

One thing which I found common between India and Australia was their appetite for technology, and by this, I do not mean technologies behind rocket science, space technology, or anything that's pure prerogative of the highbrows. Every day, when I am on the roads or in the tram or just anywhere else, there's a certain specific way I see people behaving. Almost every person had their head lowered and eyes looking down. If one did not go beyond their faces, it would appear that human beings are structurally designed to have their heads in that position, not until we turn our gaze towards their hands and see a smartphone or tablet proudly sitting there.

We have paid a price for technology. We have traded our freedom for luxury in our lives.

People across the globe have become smartphone and tablet addicts. I was so consumed by the discovery of this pattern across the globe that I could not contain my excitement any more. I made a mental note of this and decided to have a discussion with Lee on it. When I reached our apartment, I couldn't find him, so I gave him a call.

Lee sent me a message saying he was out for some work and might get late. I was a bit disappointed because I was bubbling with so many ideas and arguments, so I decided it was best to put it down on a paper. I took my notebook and wrote what I thought I wanted to share with Lee.

When Lee came back to the apartment at around 8 p.m., I handed him my notebook and waited to see his reaction. Lee flipped through the pages and, to me, seemed quite interested in reading what I had scribbled on the paper.

Dear Faceple and Tweeple,

Hope you are enjoying the dynamic life of your metaphysical electronic world and sharing some very insightful thoughts with the rest of the not-so-connected real section of the world. I have always admired the unceasing enthusiasm with which you live and spread your infectious effervescence while clocking the time.

From the past few days, I have not been feeling well, and I blame it all on you. With your unfading energy and ever-happening life, my enthusiasm and optimism seem to fall below the quintessential mark, and it's now that I have decided to pour some of my precious and highly confidential thoughts to you.

I have often wondered about the almost mass hysterical impact created by certain sudden phenomenal things in life. It seems as though we have all been born on earth with a single-minded dedication to endorse those things and eat, sleep, and drink them with every passing moment of our lives.

Few days back, I was asked by a very dear friend of mine, via an email, if I was enjoying a good health or not. After my assurance that I was hale and hearty, I became curious to know what made him worry about my health, and his plain and unpretentious reply came as 'You have not been active on Facebook for a while, so I was wondering if you have fallen sick!'

Someone had once said that the world is shrinking, but who knew that the wide network of webs will act as catalyst in further hastening this process. There are millions of websites on the Internet today, and now, almost every Tom, Dick, and Harry can boast of a web page belonging to him and her!

I was under the impression that social networking sites were meant for connecting with our friends and keeping the concept of keep-in-touch alive in a less formal manner. But I was hopelessly wrong. My silly brain did not know that these websites are more casual form of *Aaj Tak* and *A Current Affair* and need reporting of everything I do or think in my day—or I would be categorised as either orthodox, introvert, antisocial, or a distasteful combination of all.

In your world, one's degree of affability is measured against how many friends you have on Facebook or how many people are following you on Twitter. Whether you actually possess a charming personality with a pleasant demeanour is, of course, entirely immaterial. Suddenly the whole equation of relationships gets changed, measured by your status on these websites. If you are seeing someone but are projected as single on Facebook, then it is only a matter of time when your love life would either get exposed to the world through some highly excited (read: bean spiller!) friend of yours or succumb to its natural death due to your inability to accept it in the public (so would your partner feel).

Don't you dare think that this networking bug has infected only our social life. While Facebook and Twitter rule the roost in our social circles, the corporate world isn't far from being sabotaged. LinkedIn has opened up platform for people for display their professional credentials, achievements, and aspirations in full public glare. For centuries, what was considered personal and confidential is now being flaunted with a dash of arrogance.

This website also allows you to massage your ego by showing off the recommendations from your colleagues, clients, and bosses! Whether you are actually hard worker with passion to learn new things and focused and detail-oriented is again reduced to the puny status. Your recruiters are happy as long as their senses are cajoled with your recommendations-oozing perfection (read: manipulations).

Some nincompoops are so smitten by social media that a day or two away from these would certainly put them on life-saving ventilators. At times, it becomes difficult to figure out whether people are actually dumb or are simply unaware of the absence of other people's interest in their lives. How else would you explain situations where they blurt out every single thought cropping up in their minds or slap every snap of their holidays and vacations on our faces! I don't care whether you went to Honolulu or Bermuda Triangle with your girlfriend or bought a sexy dress at discounted price from DFO or had a new haircut. How on earth would your homegrown tomatoes or garden peas stir up my soul when a picture of your latest tequila shots in some glitzy pub could not invigorate my mind to say the least?

It is quite amusing when people report every breath that they take on such websites and then cry foul about the privacy issues haunting them. Gone are the good old days when mails or even emails formed the basis for exchanging pleasantries and a phone call would just be a gratifying event. If you have not wished your friends on their birthdays, anniversaries, promotions, and weddings on these sites, then you certainly don't care for them! So what if you wished them in person? A public display of affection is a must to reaffirm your continuity in that relationship.

How much is too much is yet to be defined for majority of us, especially for the class of people who aren't yet clear about the boundaries of networking and bombarding!

While I am confident that the population from my part of the world would continue to drift towards your part, I am also hoping that few crazy souls from your world would get some sanity into their heads and join our side of the world to echo my sentiments and prevent the concept of real from blurring into surreal.

I look forward to hear from you soon (not immediately).

Yours sincerely,
Reaple (Real People)

'So what do you have to say?' I asked Lee after he handed back the book to me.

'Well, I think you are right, and although I keep shifting my base from being a Faceple/Tweeple to Reaple, I guess the challenge lies in striking a right balance. Don't forget that these social media tools have helped people connect to their long-lost friends and near and dear ones and contributed a lot in raising social awareness about various issues.' Lee said all this in one breath, and although I did not disagree to all his points, I felt stronger for what I had written.

'I think you must get this published in our uni magazine.' Lee looked smilingly at me.

'No way! This was just for our discussion and not meant to be published,' I said in disbelief.

'Leave that to me, Sushi. If you have no objection, I will get it through into our uni magazine. I think people would like to read such stuff. It's cool, and we can all relate to it,' Lee said nonchalantly, but his voice had certain assertiveness and caring tone to it that I gave in to his demand.

'Okay, let me first edit it and add more substance to it in that case. I will give it back to you in the morning.' I high-fived Lee, beaming with smile and honestly feeling quite amused at my own skills of translating my incoherent thoughts into articulate and intelligible written paragraphs.

After that day, I would keenly look out for our uni magazines to check if my article was published or not and had made dozens of trip to the library just to get a sneak peek into how these articles look in the magazines. I would just flip the pages and imagine my name and photo in the features section.

It was also during one of my clandestine visits to our library when I chanced upon an article which talked about the final death of the telegram system in India—perhaps the oldest form of communication used if one ignored the well-trained pigeons, which for decades had carried the responsibility of acting as the sole channel of communications between two ardent lovers or kings who were at loggerheads or their ministers and several other minions.

Most of us have seen and experienced the sea change in the ways of communication, especially over the last decade. With the burgeoning of emails on the horizon of technology, the previous tools like letters and telegrams had already become outdated, but what is even more fascinating is the latest trend where one can feel the gradual fading out of emails with the advent of smartphones, WhatsApp, Skype, Viber, and loads of other techno apps and software. What is exhilarating is the fact that most of these tools are either free or have nominal usage fee. The long hours of trunk call bookings have given way to instant messaging and chatting, and to make up for the absence of tones and expressions in our voices, we now have *emoticons.*

Anyone from my generation and under are well versed with using these emoticons, which have expanded to include small icons for veggies, cars, buildings, and bundles of other icons apart from the regular smiley faces with various human moods and expressions.

Whether you are feeling happy, disgruntled, low-spirited, blessed, curious, amazed, shocked, loved, or anything else in the different faculties of the mind, then be rest assured that you can communicate that to your folks without writing/typing a single letter/number. I love how we can just add emoticons to our messages and express ourselves more effectively. The constant inclusion of smileys in our online conversations has tuned our minds so much to these visual expressions that they have become a sort of must-have now. Try sending someone a text saying 'I am happy for you' without a happy emoticon, and both the sender and receiver of that message would feel something amiss from the text.

The impact created by these smileys emoticons is far-fetched and has deeper connection with our senses. Initially perceived as just cool, these emoticons have become a must-have, a trend which has been boosted with the smartphone usage. So what do you do next when you want to go for drinks, dinner, or partying with friend? Send a long text message or just a couple few keywords with appropriate emoticons, and voila! Your message is ready to be sent and delivered. While most friends like it, there are others who find it difficult to get used to this concept of using smileys for various purposes.

Emoticons are catchy, fun, quirky, and direct, apart from the fact that they can be used independent of text messages. Well, most of them certainly can be. Many people argue that smileys are indeed an effective way of communication as they help to plug in the gap of visual expressions which gets created while typing a text message of writing an email. Smileys are here to stay, and this got validated by *Oxford Dictionaries* blog, which bestowed the honour of word of the year 2015 to a smiley depicting a face with tears of joy. However, it is important that we know when and where to use these emoticons to avoid any modern-day technology faux pas. Like most of the communication tools, emoticons too can make or break your relationships if you are careless with them and show signs of non-verbal diarrhoea.

So next time when I wanted to express my happiness, I had two choices: 'I am happy' or ☺ ☺ ☺.

Chapter 6

To Mom with Love

We were getting late for one of our early morning lectures one day, and Lee had left in even more hurry than me for the class. I had woken up very late despite Lee's repeated attempts, so I told him I would join him later. A little while later, I got a call on my cell phone.

'Mate, I forgot my notebook for the lecture. Could you please pick it up on your way to the class?' Lee said in a panting voice.

'Yeah, sure. Where can I find it?' I blurted out while rubbing my eyes and struggling hard to make sense of what Lee was uttering on the other end.

'Ah . . . I can't remember now, but it should be somewhere on my bed or in the drawer of the side table. Just look up there, mate. You know where I usually sit in the room,' Lee murmured, sounding confused and in utter hurry.

'Okay, no worries. I will get it for you,' I said this to calm him down while making a mental note of his request.

After Lee hung up, I went straight to his bedside table and looked through it completely, but there were no signs of any book or notebook. It was hard to say that this bedside table belonged to a student. I next looked at his bed. Lee's bed was generally left in a typical fashion after he woke up in the morning.

The bed sheet bore an almost crumbled and wrinkled look from one side, and I often wondered how he managed to do that. Anyway, pushing my thoughts away, I looked around on his bed. There was nothing on top of the quilt, so I lifted it up to see if there was something underneath it, and I did find two notebooks. I picked them up, and just when I was about to leave, my eyes fell on the yellow corner of a notebook which was peeping from under his pillow. I didn't know which one he wanted, so I picked up all the three notebooks and sprinted towards the uni after getting myself in a presentable shape.

I wasn't sure if I could make it to the uni before the lecture actually got over. As soon I reached the class, Lee was happy to see me and snatched away two notebooks from the bundle that was in my hand. After the lecture got over, we dashed outside for some coffee as I was still sleepy.

Just then, Lee's cell phone rang, and he got on to the call while signalling to me that he would join me shortly. Having nothing better to do, I started sauntering in the well-manicured lawn just outside our class. After a minute or two, I got bored and sat on the grass and began flipping through the pages of the notebooks in my hand to kill some time. Just then, my eyes read something which felt out of place. I checked the cover of the notebook, and it had Lee's name scribbled on it clearly. I flipped few pages to read those lines again, although I knew I was wrong in doing so. I read what appeared like a diary entry to me.

My mom couldn't speak English, and I was ashamed of that.

She also never wore high heels, lipsticks, and stylish watches like my other friends' mothers.

When I was in school, I used to get embarrassed when my mother would talk in Mandarin with my teachers while all my friends' parents would blabber in English. I used to shut my ears and secretly wish to run away from there. Gradually, I started requesting my father to come to my school alone for any function. I knew this pained my mom, but I was more bothered about my reputation than her feelings.

It was a big relief for me when I finished my junior high school and entered high school life as I knew there would be no parent–teacher meetings in high school and I wouldn't be obliged to see my mother grappling with English in her old-fashioned avatar covered in cheongsam.

Not that I did not love her, but I was ashamed to bring her into my social life. After all, I too had a reputation to live by. As years passed by, my interaction with my mom began to diminish while I flourished in life. After completing my high school, I took up a part-time but decently well-paying job in a metro city and started inching closer towards my dream. I would call up my parents once or twice in a month and exchange pleasantries. My father was a man of few words, and our relationship was quite formal. My mother, on the other hand, loved talking, but I did not love listening to her pure-Mandarin lectures all the time, so I would talk very briefly with her. I could sense a tone of disappointment in her voice when I would say 'I will call you later', but I chose to ignore it. After all, mothers are used to playing their emotional cards all the time.

I reduced my trips to home from four times to two times in a year, mostly on Chinese New Year and Christmas. Even on these occasions, I would spend most of my time either catching up with old friends or watching television. My mother, on the other hand, would glow with happiness on my arrival and prepare the most elaborate feast for every meal while I stayed there, which was not more than three days each time. I admit that I used to love her preparations when I was a child but not any more. I had grown weary of her cooking style, and on many occasions, I had been generous enough to pour out my feelings to her.

'Mom, I can't eat this. Why have you added so much chilli to this dish?' or 'It smells awfully of garlic.' I would rant about her cooking with such statements.

'But *zongzi* is your favourite dish, son.'

'It *was*. Not any more, Mom,' I would say irritatingly. 'You guys don't even know me properly.'

I am not sure if my mom cried after that, but I saw her wiping the corners of her eyes when she came to call me back for lunch. She had made some fresh-steamed buns for me. I didn't want to go, but I was hungry, so I went and ate half-heartedly. This had almost become a routine until last year when my mother stopped preparing a feast for supper and cooked food only after checking my preferences. I was happy, but I was not sure about my mother.

During these days, she would talk to me about things like my graduation, my health, and what was happening in and around my life. I would listen to her, nod my head a few times, and respond with some words to feel satisfied that I have spent time with her. Three years passed after that. I did not go to a grad school as I was too busy galloping in my jobs. Whatever little conversation I had was with my father.

On the pretext of being busy, my conversations with Mom grew from few to fewer and almost negligible in the present scenario. Once, I got a call on my work landline. The receptionist informed me that it was my mom on the line. I grew very annoyed with her. I picked up the phone, and as soon as I heard my mom on the other side, I took out all my anger on her and almost screamed at her for calling me at my work and ordered her not to use this number again.

It was six months after that, and I had become too busy in my world. I had not spoken to my mom even once in these six months, although I used to get her news from Dad in his two-word description 'She's fine', and I didn't want to know more than that.

It was not until this morning when I got a call from Dad saying that Mom had died that I began to think of her more than I did usually. I was shocked, but I could not feel much pain. I took a flight at the first instance and reached home within four hours. Dad was still in the hospital with my mother's dead body.

I looked at her face. She wore her unfashionable demeanour with utter calmness now. I just felt sorry for her. Just then, Dad touched my shoulder and handed over a piece of paper to me. He said it was my mother's wish list of all the things which she had wanted to do in the last few years:

- Learn English.
- Learn to cook pasta and try broccoli.
- Start wearing pants and shirt.
- Learn to use mobile phone.
- Shorten my hair.

I was looking at this sheet with teary eyes. Everything on her wish list was what I had rebuked her for in the past years. I hated her as she embarrassed me with her broken English and orthodox appearance, but today I was standing with the biggest vacuum in my heart. Six months ago, she had called me up in my office just to make me hear her talk in English. She had learnt English just to make me proud of her, but today my head hung in grief, shame, and irrevocable regret for a lifetime. I have died a thousand deaths since then, but I can never get my mother back in my life.

I felt something wet on my cheek, and as I moved up my hand to feel it, I realised there were teardrops which had swelled from my eyes and started rolling down my cheek as I read along this diary entry. I suddenly felt a vortex of emotions in my heart and a deep sorry for Lee.

My mind inadvertently went back to my mother, and suddenly I was missing her very badly, including her cajoling manners, her undiluted love, and unflinching concern for me.

Although there was no similarity in what Lee had written in his diary to my mom, everything about my mom started appearing very dear to me. I made up a mental note to call her up today and let her know that I loved her and missed her sometimes. I didn't want her to feel that I cannot do without her or that I had already become devoid of emotions either.

'Sorry, Sushant! That phone call took more time than I thought. Let's go for the coffee, mate,' Lee said this while walking towards me, so I quickly closed all the notebooks. I definitely didn't want him to know that I had read his diary. At least not right now.

'No worries, mate. Hope all's well. Oh, by the way, looks like this one is yours as well.' I didn't want to bring his notebook into too much attention, so I casually passed it to him and started walking towards the coffee shop with him. Something had changed inside me that day. I began to look at relationships in a different light. Uncertainty of life had never hit me so hard before.

'Where are you lost, mate? What do you want?' Lee was asking me, pointing to the list of coffees at the counter. I hadn't realised that we had already reached the cafe so soon. I brushed aside all my thoughts and ordered for a hot chocolate, lest Lee started probing me. We took our orders and went back to the uni for the rest of the lectures for the day.

By now, I had also learnt this magical Aussie word which had made it easier for me to approach someone new. *Mate* is one word which built this bridge across two people, just like the words *bhaisaab* or *behenji* in India. In India, any male outside our family became a *bhaisaab*, and any female not related to us became a *behenji*. The man at the grocery store, *dhobiwala*, *doodhwala*, or even the man selling veggies on handcart or the hawkers on the road—collectively they could be categorised as *bhaisaabs*—or *behenjis* if they are women instead.

Similarly, *mate* is also an instant Aussie way of forging relationship with people who otherwise do not fall within the purview of our relatives, distant relatives, or family. Although in India, gone are the days when *bhaisaab* and *behenji* reflected a gesture full of respect and good manners. Nowadays, these terms are nothing less than the act of throwing an insult or making a mockery.

Elderly people might still use these words for camaraderie purposes, but for young people, it's a polite way of saying 'You lack a sense of fashion and style' or 'You are not charismatic enough' or maybe 'You belong to my parents' generation', and so it's no wonder that we dread being addressed by these terms.

My initial awkwardness at approaching people in Melbourne had slowly diminished with the generous *mateship* which, thankfully, I had picked up well on time.

After mateship, if there's one thing which makes every Aussie take pride in being an Australian, it is their Vegemite. Vegemite is a salt-rich spread prepared from beer brew, yeast, and scores of other stuff and mostly eaten with bread for breakfast, lunch, or even snacks. It's like the quintessential *dhaniya* chutney of the Indian kitchen—fits well with any supper and equally well for in-between hunger pangs.

You are not a true-blue Aussie until you have tasted and relished this iconic food item. If you are particularly not a fan of vegemite, chances are you might have to acquire the taste, just like how you do for scotch, vodka, and tequila. Well, let's say if Javed Jaffrey had to describe vegemite, I am sure he would have agreed to love to say 'It's different'. And those of my Aussie friends who did not love vegemite showcased their patriotism through footy. Do not mistake it for some kind of a refreshing pulpy fruit drink the way I did when I first came across this term. Footy is the Australian love for football combined with their laziness. But dare you not belittle this fiercely popular game here, which by the way is also played with hands.

Although cricket and golf are also quite popular in this country, footy is to Australia what cricket is to India and soccer is to Brazil—a religion. You've got to trust me on this for the absolute level of fanaticism which comes out during each footy match, especially during AFL season. Each time I watched footy games with my friends, I was reminded of several games like kabaddi, football, and boxing in the same frame by the sheer virtue of its aggressiveness.

Month 4

Chapter 7

I Finally Did It

One day our lectures finished a little earlier than expected as our prof had to rush home to attend some emergency, so we pretty much had the whole day to us. I was thinking about catching up with Kris so that all three of us could have some fun time.

'Sushi boy, what are your plans?' I heard Lee's voice which came somewhere from behind me. It was as though he had sensed what I was thinking about. Lee was walking towards me while his eyes were completely glued to his smartphone.

'Hmm . . . nothing much, I was just thinking . . .'

'You think too much! Trust me, you need to learn to conserve your brain.' Lee said this while breaking out into a small laughter.

'If there's nothing particularly planned at your end, why don't you come along with me? I will show you the gym in our uni. You could actually use it for your benefit,' Lee said with a look which to me appeared like a disapproving look. I became a little conscious and pulled down my T-shirt, almost stretching it beyond its aesthetic looks to make sure I wasn't looking like some fool.

Lee perhaps sensed my thoughts and pulled my hand and dragged me along with him. The gym was at the extreme end of the uni, and there were good chances that I would have never discovered it on my own. It was a medium-sized room with a variety of exercise machines, of which I was only aware of the treadmills, cross-trainers, and cycles. Other machines were visually familiar to me, but I had never bothered to know their names while I was in India. Lee gave me a small tour of the room, updated me about the typical gym dos and don'ts, and lastly, gave a small demo of how to use each machine. They were massive machines that looked like the Terminator or Iron Man which were fitted with small LCD screens. Our entire uni was Wi-Fi enabled, which meant I could watch my favourite videos while working out. Now that was a huge motivation for gym virgins like me.

Lee was a slender guy, like I mentioned earlier, but he was certainly well-toned and looked fit. I wasn't bad either, but I was never really conscious about my looks as I was now. I was thin and perhaps too thin; because of which, I looked a little younger than my age. I decided to use this gym facility, primarily, since it wasn't costing me anything on my pocket and, secondarily, because I really wanted to look fit, just like Lee.

I started coming to the gym on a regular basis and had learnt how to perform those exercises which I had initially seen only on televisions. After becoming a regular at the uni gym, I wondered if it was just me who thought that we, as a community, suddenly become health-conscious when we set our foot outside our country or if others also shared my bewilderment. Not that I see anything wrong with it, but I just wondered about what awakens our senses in this particular area. It's like we find some kind of magic mirror and each time when we ask it 'Mirror, mirror on the wall, am I the fittest of all?' pat comes the reply: 'No.'

For some people, this not only shatters their long-term belief of being slim and slender but also tramples their confidence in no time. The aftermath of this turns most of these people into calorie-burning machines who perennially shout, 'Oh my god, I am so fat!' Any sight of desserts, fried snacks, carbohydrates, cheese, butter, and anything oily repels them with great force, and their mainstay strictly revolves around soups, salads, oats, skimmed milk, and occasional bites of lean meat and chicken.

Such people also become unleashed when they get opportunities to satiate their timeless suppressed cravings for these food items when no one else is watching them. After all, a crime committed when no one's watching often doesn't leave much room for guilt. This is then followed by their rants: 'I over ate', 'I am feeling sick', or 'I think I am gonna puke!' People in this category are never happy with the way they look, which is mostly fuelled by their self-comparison with the well-toned blokes and sheilas from Down Under.

However, this isn't the case with everyone. There are many of us who take pride in their love handles, muffin tops, and bingo wings. Now before you arouse your sweet tooth or tickle your fascinations for KFC chicken wings, let me inform you that these terms are pure euphemistic ways to point out at the tyre around your waist, the bulging tummy over your jeans, and the dangling layer of fat from your upper arms. Ah! What a f(l)ab way to make you feel good about yourself. These people never miss any opportunity to dig into chicken *tikkas*, mutton *biryani*, or *chhole puri*, and a mouthful of *gulab jamun* or *rasmalai* is a must-have for them on top of all these goodness. They consider any form of exercise a straight insult to their well-guarded prosperity and growth. Neither the fitness spree in India nor the health consciousness of Australians can move their muscles.

In between these two extremes lies a segment of people which is horribly entangled in its perception of fitness and believes in flexing the brawns more than the brains. They love their daily workouts and gym routines just to add a bit of flamboyance to their otherwise unnoticeable personalities. This is also done in a bid to appear hep and happening amongst their fair-skinned friends and colleagues.

Then there are those for whom going to the gym and fitness centre is like going to a temple presided over by their demigods like Sallu Bhai, Arnie, or even the invincible Rock where 'Bulk up, hulk up' becomes their ultimate mantra.

Apart from such varieties of common people, there are some famous personalities too who keep me amused with their thoughts. If articles and interview excerpts from celebrities (actors, fitness gurus) are anything to go by, then the entire process of workout and gym regimes are completely out of the common man's reach. Their recommendations in fitness, diet, and choice of equipment are often on the expensive and exotic side which are tailor-made to leave a heavy dent in your pocket.

I often wondered why people didn't choose to brisk-walk or jog in the parks; rather, they splurge money on those fancy products from teleshopping. I still haven't found my answer. Well, I will have enough time to ponder over such issues after I go back to India.

After my initial awe and shock over gym and the types of people associated with it, I had time to think about myself and focus more on my well-being. I wanted to look fitter when I went back to India. This could inevitably give me another area where I could be better than my friends there.

'Lee, can you show me some chest press and abs exercises in the gym?' I asked Lee with a hope that Lee could pave the way of a fitter body for me.

'Yeah, sure I can, but have you met Mr Nair today?'

'No, why?'

'He wanted all of us to prepare a ten-minute presentation of some topic, so if you haven't met him, please do so tomorrow.'

'Damn it!' I hated public speaking even though it meant in the confines of my classroom. 'What topic did you get?' I could sense a herald of trouble coming along my way.

'I don't remember exactly, but I think it's something called glass ceiling.'

'What's that? Architecture related?'

'I have got no idea, mate. I will know tomorrow when I start preparing for it,' Lee announced with a wink.

'Cool! I will see Mr Nair tomorrow. Don't know what topic he would give me.' I said with some trepidation in my voice. I was doubly terrified—first of public speaking and second of the anonymity around the topic itself.

'Develop your SQ. That's your topic, Sushant' were the words of wisdom from Mr Nair, one of my professors, to me when I met him the next morning. It sounded too familiar to me, but I still couldn't decode what he meant by SQ. Perhaps it was some kind of a new computer language or a new tool being taught in Australian universities. Maybe my prof forgot that it was SQL and not SQ! The age-old existing languages were not Greek and Latin to me, but fathoming something new in this field could be a challenge. Luckily, I did not vocalise my thoughts and buried them in some grey cells in my brain.

'Aweready [accented version of *all right*] then. See ya on Monday. Think over how you would achieve your SQ,' my prof told me. He was of Indian origin, now settled in Australia and perhaps might even be an Aussie citizen. He always made a point to reflect that through his accent.

'Sure, Mr Nair.' I had no option but to make him feel that he was very clear in defining his requirements to me. I couldn't say no. After all, I didn't want to appear dumb to him.

'Have a nice weekend. See you on Monday,' said my prof, and with that I zoomed out of his office.

Phew!

I heaved a sigh of relief. The thought of weekend had blinded me towards everything else, so I pushed that stupid-sounding SQ out of mind for a while. I packed my bag hurriedly and dashed out of the uni. This was only after ensuring that my prof had left and that I had no further classes in the day. After reaching home, I collapsed on the bed as if I had returned from a war. Lee and Kris were busy with some chore, so I had the entire day to myself. I was feeling good. I prepared a cup of hot ginger tea and made myself comfortable on my bed with today's newspaper. I was feeling very relaxed now. Don't know whether it was the ginger tea's therapeutic effect or the feeling of weekend. Whatever it was, I was feeling calm and soothed.

As I was flipping the pages of the paper, my eyes fell on an article in the editorial section, my favourite section. It read 'Leaders and Quotients'. I started to read it and found it very engrossing up until I reached a point where they had mentioned about various quotients like intelligence, emotional, and spiritual. That meant IQ, EQ, and SQ.

So was this the SQ Mr Nair was referring to—spiritual quotient? It was yet again my turn to be gobsmacked. Now who on earth had invented this, and why do I need to develop it? I considered myself fairly intelligent enough to understand above-average complexities in my projects. I said 'above average'. This bars geeky, rote, telegraphic representations of several computer languages. Anyway, now that I knew what SQ stood for, I thought of knowing about it and the ways to develop it. The newspaper said SQ is the capability to look beyond. Now look beyond what? Trying to understand the purpose of life and the best way to serve the distressed are qualities that are found normally in a mother who understands the needs of her children. I wonder how something that sounded so uncomplicated would be complicated to implement. Being able to understand and exhibit high IQ and EQ was a challenge in itself, and now we were further being burdened with this concept of SQ. How I wish at this moment that all researchers could be put for hibernation till eternity. One day they come up with some study saying that eating XYZ is good for your health as it would lower your risk of getting a heart attack. Other day some other study would reveal that the same XYZ would cause problems to a particular body part if consumed in excess. This took me back to the old tomato ketchup advertisement where a villain had tied up the hero and ordered his henchmen, saying, '*Isko* liquid nitrogen *me dal do . . .* nitrogen *isko jeene nahin dega aur oxygen isko marne nahin dega.*' I felt comparable to that hero in the advertisement. These researchers would not let you die, nor would they let you live. Nevertheless, I still had to grapple to understand this concept. I brushed aside all thoughts from my mind and sat down with the paper which said, 'Spiritual intelligence touches the heart, mind, and the spirit. When a leader develops high degree of spiritual intelligence, the organisation will definitely excel.'

Chapter 8

What Do You Do for a Living?

I t was a usual day at the uni, and we were attending a lecture on 8085 when suddenly it started to pour heavily outside. Within no time, the sunny and vibrant Melbourne had turned grey. I was always fascinated with how, during my small stay in Melbourne, I had seen it acquire fifty shades of grey, albeit in a different fashion. The actual grey colour hovered over the mindscapes of Melburnians all throughout the year. It is a known fact that people of Melbourne love black colour, and a living testimonial to this is the daily sea of people walking on the CBD roads each morning—some heading towards their workplace while others just kicking off their shopping and fun day out—all gracefully draped in black. Second to this is Melbourne's relationship with grey colour, and I am not talking about clothes.

The long grey snake-like roads which wriggle through the CBD towards the suburbs get an unabashed companionship in the form of clusters of grey-hued clouds, which are perennially raring to pour their love upon us. Grey is like a hangover of black colour for Melburnians—only this one they love, plus it does not require a dose of Panadol to disappear.

Come winter, which is nearly three-fourth of the Melbourne weather, or rainy season, which stays there in its thick and thin, the aura around the city becomes grey. It acquires a glowing silver halo shining over the city formed at the horizon by the beautiful commingling of grey roads and grey skies. Some find this sight a bit depressing, but to me, it reflects the ultimate spirit of this city—a city which never gives up and shines through even the most distressed situations. Amongst all facets of grey, the one which I love the most is when the clouds turn grey from pristine cottony white, and Melbourne gets its fresh and invigorating look with each downpour. I learnt from my local mates that it was not long ago when Melbourne was marred with the downside of grey colour with the bushfire, and each year, some unfortunate ones get engulfed in this tragedy. The scattered ashes belched out the anger and frustration of this city, resulting from the scorching heat of summers, and told a heart-rending tale of some destroyed lives and some broken hearts—but this is life as they say.

If you are in CBD, it's hard to miss the sight of grey here. Be it the concrete for the buildings or the mixture of tar and pebbles on the roads, there is no way you could escape the wondrous sight of this colour wherever your eyes roved.

If you go by the dictionary definition of grey colour, it is rather defined as one of the neutral colours, apart from black and white; however, to me it depicts much more than that. It depicts the freshness of rain, the excitement of something coming to existence, the newness of our ambience, and the optimism that our tomorrow would be better than our today. From roads to sky, from low to high, Melburnians love these shades of grey. So what if these are lesser than fifty shades?

There was no gainsaying the fact that grey was very much a Melbourne colour irrespective of the way you view it.

I felt a nudge on my elbow and came out of my reverie. Lee looked at me as though I was sleeping in the class. I looked at my watch, which showed we still had twenty minutes of class left. With great difficulty, I pulled myself back into the class. After all, the only reason I came to Melbourne was my studies and not its shades of grey.

Lee once took me to his friend's BBQ party where I met a girl, and during our conversation, I was quite impressed to learn that she was working as a fashion consultant at some clothing line store in the CBD. She was around my age, and to work as something like her was an indication of her brilliant mind and skills. At first, I thought it might be another term for fashion designer, but on further probing (thanks to my curious nature), I decoded the roles and responsibilities behind her lofty designation of fashion consultant. Well, let's just say that she did what the salesperson in a clothing store would do in India.

For me, this understanding did not demean her work; rather, it brought out a very striking observation within my purview—her pride and her confidence in her work. Eventually, I came across several such fancy designations during my stay in Melbourne, most of which are virtually unheard of in India.

For instance, if you are working in a hair salon and enjoy trimming, cutting, and chopping other people's hair, then you can call yourself a hair specialist/expert rather than a barber or a beautician or a hairstylist. Similarly, people who clean, polish, and wax cars can boastfully call themselves car detailers instead of just mechanics. Likewise, you can also be a roofing specialist, a sparkie (electrician), or a chippie (carpenter) and perform your daily chores to fix problems in other people's house and lead a luxurious lifestyle.

Life is even better if you are a miner in Australia. If the haggard and suppressed look of a miner popularised by Amitabh Bachchan in the movie *Kala Patthar* evoked sympathy in our hearts, then get ready to feel envious of the Aussie miners, who are ensured a rich lifestyle with not more than twenty days of work per month, alongside perks which are capable of turning even the CEOs in India green with envy.

It often amused me how as a child we were taught the concept of dignity of labour but how conveniently we forget about it when it comes to practice. Jobs which are considered menial in India are the ones which actually fetch you big moolah in this part of the world. IT is no more the big ticket to money and happiness in Australia; rather, it is the blue-collar jobs which can make you movers and shakers in this country.

If you are a television buff, then you must have surely seen one of the reality shows like *Master Chef*, *The Block*, *Farmer Wants a Wife*, and many others which hail the blue-collar professionals from different fields. Not that I had the privilege to watch these programmes, but occasionally, I would catch their glimpse or read about them on the news website or overhear enthusiastic people in trams and trains discussing each episode in detail with passion. The difference between white- and blue-collar jobs sublimes with fancy designations and comfortable lifestyle, which people from each category enjoy here. Another factor which helps in maintaining the equality between these two pedestals is the absence of language barrier. People from all walks of life, all strata of the economy, and all parts of Australia are stitched together by one common language—English. Dignity of labour is thus not difficult to preach and practise here.

This realisation was a turning point in my life—a moment when I no more felt ashamed of my part-time job of a dishwasher. I decided to call up my mom and dad and inform them about my job. After all, it was my first hard-earned money, and I wanted them to know that I was living my life in a responsible way in Australia. Although my parents were taking care of my expenses, I did not want them to even think for a moment that I might be whiling away my time in the sun, sand, and surf Down Under.

While a rich girl marrying a cab driver/waiter may be a super hit formula for success in Hindi films, in Australia such disparity in professions is a reality and a much-accepted social norm. I have chanced upon acquaintances where one partner has a PhD in mathematics while the other one is a truck driver, one partner is a business analyst in a bank, while the other is a landscaper. I was out of my wits end when I learnt about such couples and then further learnt that it's absolutely normal in Australian social fabric to support such liaisons.

It was only much later that I discovered that in Australia a professional qualification is a not a prerequisite for someone to earn big moolah. I hope and wish that someday we too would be able to replicate this model of respect and appreciation towards work in India.

Month 5

Chapter 9

Population, Preparation, and Pollution

'Let's go for a walk, mate. I am feeling too sleepy,' Lee said to me with the sound of utter boredom in his voice.

'Hmmm, where do you want to go?'

'Nowhere special. Just some casual aimless walk. I want to get some fresh air.'

'Okay, how about we go to the park outside the Victoria Library and eat our lunch?'

'Perfect! I can get some air and some sleep too, and you can read your books.'

'I don't think I will read any book until I eat something.'

'Oh yes! Let's eat, man. Maybe I can sleep better after that.'

We grabbed some lunch from outside our uni and walked towards the park. Lee finished his lunch while walking and crashed on the park grass as soon as we reached there.

I did not like eating while walking, so I held on to my lunch and began nibbling only when I found the right spot to sit.

It was a cold morning, but the sudden appearance of sun at noon had turned the day more pleasant, and so it wasn't a surprise that people had flocked outside to get their quota of sunshine on their skin. With Lee resting beside me with his eyes closed, I didn't realise when and how I got consumed by the constant commotion of people and trams across the street. Everybody seemed to be heading somewhere as if they all had something specific, something important to look forward to in their lives. My chain of thoughts took me back and forth between Australia and India, and that's when I suddenly recalled the three *P*s which were a quintessential part of my growing-up days. There are some words which just get ingrained in your mind as you grow up. In my case, there were plenty of such words, few of which were terms like *population*, *preparation*, and *pollution*.

It was weird that all these words had developed with a negative connotation in my psyche, but much of this had to do with the fact that I had spent all my life in India up until a few months ago. It's amazing how the relevance of a subject assumes a different perception if the context is changed. In my case, the change of context was from India to Australia.

When I was in school, we used to read about how India is about to explode on the population graph, and within a few years' time, this big bang theory had actually become a reality. We had crossed the dreadful figure of billion, and population indeed had become a war zone. From being touted as the primary cause of poverty and unemployment, population had become the favourite scapegoat for literally everyone's bad performance, including our government. If China was considered a role model with its 'one child per couple' theory, our government too tried hard to promote '*Chhota parivar, Sukhi parivar*'.

In short, population was bad, or so I thought, till I came to Australia. The idea of having four kids per couple is not only a dream of every Aussie family—which by the way also includes a house with big backyard, two dogs, and one car—but also a big blow to my belief of unpopularity of population in this country. 'The more the merrier' is the policy here, and this is how my notion around my first *P* completely went down the drain.

The four main metro cities of India individually can challenge the whole of Australia in terms of its human population. People here sometimes cannot fathom how we Indians even manage to get along in our day-to-day life with at least someone else always breathing up on our necks on roads in public transports and in shopping stores. At my end, in Melbourne, I would inadvertently start counting the number of people who could have easily slipped into the space which stays unoccupied when I look at the roads, malls, and public transports. Perhaps this is also one reason why I have never been able to understand what it meant whenever I overheard people discussing about traffic jams on some roads and some bridges, particularly on Melbourne's West Gate Bridge.

To come out of my state of disbelief, I decided to focus on my second *P*, *preparation*. Films like *3 Idiots* and *Taare Zameen Par* have done it—not preparation so to say. They have made it a common rhetoric to talk about the 'too much' academic pressure in our schools. Right from the first standard, we get into the grind of preparations—every month for the internal tests, every three months for the unit tests, every six months for the semester exams, and every year till twelfth to score high in board exams. Phew! This is only stage 1. Stage 2 is all about the rat race to secure great GPAs and campus placements in colleges, but isn't this every Indian's story, at least of those who get to go to school. After numerous stages of such preparations, I came to Australia, and to my surprise, this term is almost alien to the students here.

With little school tasks, few courses, and fewer assessments, how would these kids even know what our definition of *preparation* meant, forget understanding it completely? Not having any exams till the ninth grade is not merely a dream of every student but a much-cherished dream too. It's unfair that only developed nations' kids got to enjoy these benefits while the underdogs like us were made to slog.

It was then I understood how my maid's child used to feel when she would sit on the floor in our house, eating a piece of bread, while we would lazily slouch on our sofas and munch on grilled sandwiches. So much for parity, huh! Nevertheless, this is how my illusion around my second *P* also got shattered. Unfortunately, the concept of no preparations is applicable only in Aussie schools. At the university levels, students again have to slog, grind, and burn the midnight oil to score good grades. I often thought I should have come here while I was a toddler and enjoyed the perks of going to the school sans any exams. Well, I was just grateful that one doesn't have to slog to daydream at least.

Now I was just left with my third *P*, *pollution*. Well, let's just say thank God, and I really mean thank God, because my belief and connotation about this *P* has remained intact even Down Under. In fact, I was extremely pleased with the way littering was considered an offence here, not to mention the systematic garbage collection process and the countless garbage bins which hardly allowed you be careless with your rubbish. It wouldn't be wrong to say that India and Indians can take a leaf out of this Aussie spirit and become more aware and responsible. Now before you ask me about air and water pollution, let me tell you that I am still looking for these two fugitives. They haven't left a trace on this land. In fact, during my few months' stay here, I had nearly forgotten the smell of the exhaust let out by vehicles and the ear-deafening honks, which are a norm on the Indian roads. If we heard someone honking on the Aussie roads, it clearly meant someone else has flouted some driving decorum.

The way two of my strong beliefs got trampled in Australia made me think if we would ever conform to the same set of thoughts, and I got my answer in our common belief about my third *P*. These three *P*s helped me unravel some fascinating aspects of Aussie life with their confusion, contradiction, and well, a bit of agreement too.

Chapter 10

Power of Questions

There are certain specific things we indulge into as kids, we indulge into as teenagers, we indulge into as married people, we indulge into as parents, as friends, and even as working professionals. We hate interrogations when it is targeted at us, but we love it when someone else is on the shooting line.

Asking questions by itself is not bad; rather, it is an art which most of us are not aware of, forget even championing this area. And I am saying this based on my vast experience of living in India, where people think it is their prerogative to shoot endless questions and interrogate others, and my small experience of living in Australia, where questions differ in their nature but, at the end of the day, are still questions, and people love to pose it to others.

In this case, I am talking about the kind of questions which lead you to believe that 'if speech is silver, silence is gold'.

As human beings, we all have the natural tendency to dislike interrogations in any form, like what, why, where, when, and how, especially the inquisitive intrusions from our so called well-wishers. I was relieved when I moved out of India, thinking that this breed would not bother me any more, but I was wrong. Be it India or Australia, such people always carry their habits wherever they go.

After undergoing a lot such gruelling session during my exchange programme, I identified three broad categories in which these (unwanted) interrogations could be roughly slotted.

Category 1: Those questions which make you pull your hair

Most of the time, this kind of question is unintentional, and people under this category state the obvious in their interrogations, like when you return home from work/shopping, your better half would ask, 'Oh! You are back?' (This is not even correct English, but we will assume we cannot find anything wrong in it.)

What you say: 'Yes, honey, I am.'

What you actually want to say: 'No, honey, I am still at work/the shop. What you are seeing is just my spirit!'

Category 2: Those questions which make you grab a dictionary of your choicest expletives

People under this category are nosy by nature. They question you about your life and its really personal aspects without realising that they are overstepping their limits or intruding into your personal space, like every unmarried man or woman around the age of twenty-eight gets asked: 'So when are you getting married?' or if already married, 'When are you guys having kids?'

What you say (with a fake smile on your face): 'As soon as I find the right person, Aunty-ji/Uncle-ji' or 'We'll plan it soon, Aunty-ji/Uncle-ji.'

What you actually want to say (with clenched teeth): 'I have decided to stay single because I do not want to end the sole purpose of your life [asking questions], you moron @#$%!' or 'Never, because we hate kids! If you are so fond of them, why don't you plan another one for yourself @#$#@!'

Category 3: Those questions which make you realise the eternity of time

People in this category love to play *Kaun Banega Crorepati* or its Aussie version *Who Wants to Be a Millionaire?* with you and ask you zillions of questions before divulging their real intentions behind those questions. With each question, you wonder what this person is really up to until you reach a point when you want to just hang up the phone after yelling a satisfactory 'Shuuuuut up!'

Picture this scene:

A: Hi! What are you guys doing?
You: Hey! Nothing much, just finishing some pending chores.
A: Okay. Are you guys planning to go out anywhere today?
You: Not really. Actually, we haven't planned anything yet. What's the matter?
A: Oh! Nothing special. We would be around your house in the evening for some work, so we were thinking of swinging by for some time.
You: That would be lovely. Come and have tea with us in the evening.
A: Yeah, sure. Why not? We would love to, if you insist.

While in reality, you would have preferred this:

A: Hi! Would you guys be free for some time this evening? We would be around in that area, so we were wondering if we could catch up with you for a while.

You: Oh! That's nice. We would be at home today, so please drop by whenever you are done with your job. Let's have some *chai pakoda* in the evening.

A: Awesome. We'll see you in the evening. Bye.

Now isn't this a short and crisp conversation where you are not left assuming about the agenda of your well-wishers.

Having said that, I loved how the students here did not hesitate in asking questions and how the teaching methodology emphasised on the real-life application of the learning in classrooms. Unlike India, where we often joked about the inverse relationship between one's knowledge and marks in exams, in Australia I found that someone getting a GPA of 4.5 actually knew stuff which just couldn't have been possible with the cram theory.

The contrasts did not stop here.

Over the period of a few months, I had gained in my memory what I had lost in my real-life experience in Australia— things which had just disappeared from my horizon after I had moved to the southern hemisphere. Absence of some of these things was greatly missed while others were a great relief in life.

It seemed like just another regular day when I realised that I hadn't boiled milk in the last one year, an act which was performed religiously on a daily basis in India. Although pasteurised milk is commonly available there as well, we were tuned to boil it first before consuming it in tea, coffee, or any other form. Ever since I had come to Australia, the milk got directly poured from its container into bowls of cornflakes, smoothies, or mugs of coffee and tea. It was as if I had woken up from a slumber and found that there was one thing less which I had to worry about—spilling of boiling milk. However, much mundane this act might have been back then, now I do miss it at times. Ah! Little joys of life, like they say.

Another thing which was conspicuous by its absence was the insect species—namely mosquitoes and houseflies. The frequent buzzing of houseflies and the irritating stings of mosquitoes, which are quintessentially associated with the rainy and summer seasons in India, have been out of our lives Down Under. There are also no frogs croaking to auger the rainy season and no chirping of crickets at night, the only companion of the utter silence of the Indian nights. The much-hated species of cockroaches which are often found patrolling the kitchens have also not obliged us ever since I bade goodbye to India. Missing these things isn't a reflection of a normal or a sane mind; nonetheless, it does take me down the memory lanes of our good old times.

Featuring next in my list were the television advertisements. I just needed a few weeks of stay in Australia to understand the lack of creativity in their television advertisements. While TV ads in India were high on creativity, presentation, and concept, the ads Down Under are bland, lack a storyline, and often are so direct that I often wondered if it was actually meant for what it showed. Who can forget those innovative Fevicol ads, the thought-provoking Idea Cellular slogan 'What an Idea, Sirji!' or the Chintamani of ICICI Bank?

Many of these advertisements have left an indelible mark on our minds, and their themes, characters, or slogans are remembered by people for ages. On the contrary, the Australian advertisements still appeared to be in their infancy and were yet to come out of age, especially when you saw a man dressed in a kilt, shouting blatantly on your screen, 'Mega liquidation sale,' prompting you to either change the channel or switch off your TV set rather than listen to his loud announcements which were hard to focus on because of his distractive dress-up.

While some of these things were sorely missed in Australia, other things were missed for reasons which were comforting. Good, bad, or ugly, the reminiscence of the past helps to create nostalgia in everyone's mind, and if not for some of these things, we wouldn't have understood our emotions for our country, our people, and that strange thing which we often call Indianness.

I missed my home and its comfort a great deal, which had always made me feel happy and secure. It felt strange, but occasionally, I did miss their questions. There was nobody in Melbourne to ask if I had my food, if I needed anything, or if just I wanted a warm hug in the cold and often lonely evenings.

Although there were just the three of us—me, my mother, and my father—living in that house, it was my first world. I loved my parents very much and perhaps in the same proportion, but the relationship I shared with each of them was very different in nature.

Everyone in our larger family believed that I was my mother's apple of the eye. She doted on me a lot like every mother dotes on her child, a fact I have used to my advantage several times in the past. She was simple, caring, and loving but had her own idiosyncrasies which drove me nuts on numerous occasions. She was a professor working at a premier university in our hometown, but her beliefs sometimes made me think that she hadn't really allowed her education and exposure to sync deeper into her mind and heart.

She was a complete God-fearing and highly religious lady for whom lighting *diya* and *agarbatti* two times a day at our home temple was mandatory, and without which her day wouldn't be complete. She loved chanting *bhajans* and *shlokas* during her prayer times, but the problem would arise when she would play those *bhajans* on our music systems during festivals. We had spoilt a lot of cassettes and CDs due to repetitive playing, but nothing could dampen my mother's enthusiasm in this regard. I am not particularly a religious person, so I never really bothered about performing all these rituals, although my mom, once in a while, would ask me to come and pray to God and seek their blessings for my *su-budhi*.

Apart from her religious side, she was a very strong lady. She had supported my father during his formative career days and stood behind him like an iron lady. My parents had a very humble start, and although my mother belonged to a very wealthy family, she had happily married my father, who did not have great riches associated with his family. Theirs was an arranged marriage. Somebody had tipped my *nanaji* about my father, saying that he would not find such an eligible boy for his daughter anywhere in the next ten villages, and this testimony was enough for my *nanaji* to zero in on my dad as a suitor for his beloved daughter.

My maternal grandfather was a very rich and reputed man. My mother was his only daughter after five sons, and there was never any doubt that everyone in his family loved and pampered my mother the most. Since both my mother and father were then still pursuing their higher studies, they continued to stay apart after their marriage. My father went back to his engineering college to complete his degree while my mother stayed back at my grandfather's place to complete her graduation.

My mother told me that my father would often visit her during his semester breaks, and that was the only time they could meet each other. It was only after my father got his first job as an engineer that he came back to my grandfather's house to formally take my mother away with him.

They had been married for five years by then, but they still hadn't felt absolutely comfortable in each other's company. My parents came to Mumbai to set up their first home after marriage, and that's when they both got to know each other better. My mother has told me on several occasions that she totally adored how my father looked after her and how happy she felt despite her fears of living in a metro city like Mumbai.

I am sure, with time, both of them got synced with this spirit and vibe of Mumbai and completed their further studies and eventually took to teaching as professors. My *nanaji* always felt that teaching was the best profession for career-seeking women as it allowed her time to still look after her family. I am not sure if that was why my mother became a professor or if she really wanted to teach. Nonetheless, she was enjoying her life, and that made me happy.

I remember the time when my mother wanted me to go to a specific school for my higher secondary classes but my dad wasn't quite keen on sending me to that school as he felt the school fees were way beyond their affordability. But my mom stood her ground and convinced my father that even if it took her to sell off her jewellery or eat into her savings, she wouldn't accept anything less for her child's education.

I don't know how they managed, but I certainly went to that school, and I must admit that I enjoyed every bit of my last five years of schooling with great friends, great teachers, and plenty of extracurricular activities. Before I came to Melbourne, I had never really looked at her the way I did when I was far, far away from her. She has been my anchor whenever I was upset or sulking. I remember how she would sit next to me on the bed and console me whenever I scored less marks in my exams.

'It's all right, *beta*. You can always try for better marks next time,' she would say with a smile on her face while patting me on my back and ruffling my hair to cheer me up. I never told her then, but I would always feel pumped up after that, as if some sort of burden would get lifted off my mind. I missed her a lot. In fact, I think I started valuing the little things she did for me to make my life comfortable and great.

My father, on the other hand, rarely showed his emotional side ever since I could remember. It wasn't that he was not affectionate or loving, but I guess over the years he had preferred keeping his emotional aspect at bay. I had a complex relationship with my father. Like my mother, my father too is a man of simplicity, and everything about him reflected that. He preferred simple clothes, home-made food, and a simple abode, and this wasn't a surprise for me, considering he was a self-made man who moved out of a small village and made a mark for himself purely based on his skills and merits. For him, education mattered a lot, and that's why perhaps he encouraged my mother to finish her studies beyond graduation and take up a profession of her choice. He loved me a lot, but as I grew up, his ways of showing his affection changed towards me. He taught me to ride a bicycle and would often tell me to exercise and be fit. However, I preferred playing outside with my friends than indulging into any kind of exercise.

I remember stories about how my dad used to hold my hand and help me walk when I was still a toddler. In the beginning, I would fall down in most of my attempts, but he was there to hold me and hug me back. I remember how I had fought with him once when I was in class 8 because he did not take us out for a vacation as promised.

That summer vacation, I was alone as most of my friends had gone out with their families. I had sulked and sulked over this matter for the entire two months. It was only when I had become a little older that I learnt from my mother that Dad couldn't take us for a vacation then because the money he had saved up for the trip was used up for my annual school camping. Before I knew this, I was certain that he considered such trips as a waste of money and didn't want to take my mother and me for a vacation. I was naive, just how other kids at my age are.

I was a brilliant student and always scored amongst top five ranks in my class until I entered high school in class 9. I was still scoring good marks, but I could never be a ranker like my old times, and I guess this pricked my father somewhere. He believed that I had stopped taking my studies seriously and that I had fallen into bad company and lost a sense of direction in life. My mother would often have conversations with him about me and try to defend me, but I could see disappointment in my father's eye—or so I thought. With time, I started drifting away from him and would hardly have any conversations with him, sometimes for days or weeks together. I felt he was not really appreciative of me, and I am not sure how he thought I felt for him.

He had a very modest upbringing as a child. His was a large family, and my grandfather was the only breadwinner to support the family. He was a principal in a school and was quite proud of my father, who excelled in studies and, despite all odds, went on to become the first engineer from his village. In his village, my father is still known as 'engineer sahab', despite the fact that over the years, there were other engineers as well. Dad provided me with everything which he thought a father should to his child—a good schooling, great home, loving ambience, and other comforts which he wasn't privileged to enjoy during his childhood. But I felt sometimes he would bring his childhood into my childhood and expect me to value these things the way he would have valued back then.

'You have become spoilt, Sushant. You don't know how lucky you are to enjoy these things and get a proper education. You must focus more on your studies,' he would growl at me in frustrations sometimes. Not that I wasn't good or interested in my studies, but the fact that he would harp on it so much made me lose my interest at times. I loved doing what other kids at my age loved. We used to play outside for hours together during our school summer vacations when we were young, then we got hooked on to the video games. I still remember my first video game, Mario. Dad never bought these things because he felt these were a waste of time and money. He bought other stuff, like some musical instrument which I was never interested in.

Now when I think back, I feel it was more of mismatch in our likings which made me feel this way about each other. We weren't wrong. We were just different people with different likings.

As I grew up, I became more interested in computers and networking stuff, most of which he didn't understand, and hence, he never genuinely appreciated my skills. He thought I was neglecting my studies and frankly speaking, my marks weren't helping me prove my point either.

Things were a far cry from the past now. I felt very differently for him. I had seen the happiness on his face when I had informed him about my selection for this exchange programme. I had heard the concern in his voice for me when I was packing for my Melbourne trip. I had seen him caring for me when we were at the airport in India. My heart now knows that no matter how he expresses himself or says things to me, deep down in his heart, my father loves me just the way I love him.

Together, my parents have always been there for me and looked after my needs and well-being. It took me a while to figure this out, but when that realisation dawned upon my sense, I knew I could not let my emotions go to waste. I decided that I when went back to India, I would tell them both how much I loved them and appreciated them for being what they had been to me. It's strange how sometimes going away from our situation helps us to understand it better and see a side which otherwise remains hidden from our everyday perspective. Perhaps that's what it means when they say distance makes the heart grow fonder.

I was not sure if it was Melbourne or just the fact that I was hundreds and thousands of miles away from them, but I had begun to see relationships in a new light. I still had views which were different from my father's and my mother's. I still had dreams which my father might not understand, but now I felt light in my head and in my heart.

Month 6

Chapter 11

Lee, Alia, and Love

It was the month of April, and the entire Indian community in my uni was buzzing due to the Indian Film Festival, which took place in Melbourne every year. People were also eagerly waiting to see Vidya Balan, whom I was told had been the brand ambassador for this festival for the past some years. I did not have any particular emotion towards Vidya Balan, but I guess my friends' eagerness had slightly rubbed off on me as I too had started looking forward to seeing her.

The other reason why this film festival was so popular amongst students was that during this time various Hindi films were screened for free for a month, and as a student, this motivation was strong enough to get crazy—irrespective of which actor or actress was cast in the movie.

On one such evening when the rest of the gang was catching up on *Barfi!* movie, I had come back to my apartment after the first half. I had already watched this movie with my college friends back in India, so I thought I could probably do much better by catching up on my lost sleep. Moreover, Lee was also not around as he had gone out to meet some other friends for a few days.

By the time I returned to my apartment, I was very tired and wanted to hit the bed. I felt too lazy to go and change, so I jumped directly on my bed and switched on the heater for a while. I pulled a blanket over my head, kept on the side, and tried closing my eyes. Something suddenly pricked me on the side of my stomach. I got up immediately and checked my jacket to find a crumpled pamphlet. I straightened it out and stretched my hand to place it on the side table, but the image on it grabbed my attention. I saw a picture of Jagjit Singh, the famous ghazal singer, on the paper. I scanned it completely and found that a Jagjit Singh concert was happening in this city on the coming Friday night. My mind raced faster. I had always wanted to attend Jagjit Singh's ghazal concert since long but could never make it happen. Now that I was miles away from my country, I couldn't let this opportunity slip out of my hand. I made up my mind to attend the concert, mostly because I loved Jagjit Singh's ghazals and also because Lee was not in the city and didn't have much plan to keep myself occupied.

'Seventy-five dollars! *Baap re!*' I exclaimed as I looked at the ticket price printed on the pamphlet. I quickly multiplied it to convert it into rupees and dropped my plan. I was on a student exchange programme and was barely managing my daily expenses; considering exchange rate was always ready to kill us. But then, within my heart, I knew how badly I had wanted to attend this concert.

I could borrow some money from Lee or Kris, or maybe I could check to see if the show had some student's concession. Several thoughts were racing through my mind without bearing any results. Suddenly I remembered my income from the part-time job I was holding on to, and I had all the reasons to smile back again. I certainly could manage seventy-five dollars; after all, I didn't splurge very often. I was justifying my decision to myself as though I was being quizzed by my parents.

Next day, I made a phone call on the number printed on the pamphlet and bought a ticket with my part-time job's income. I was feeling proud of myself, although this wasn't my first purchase from my part-time income. I eagerly waited for the whole week to pass by. On Friday evening, I wore my favourite purple shirt and matched it up with a pair of black denims. Then I slipped into my only leather jacket and saw myself in the mirror. I was very pleased with the way I was looking. I had always felt confident about my dressing sense, and this was one occasion which bolstered my belief. Feeling all pumped up about the evening, I left my apartment. I hopped into a tram from the nearest tram stop and reached the concert venue just on time.

I entered the function hall which was booked for the ghazal concert. It was a massive function hall, well organised and decorated to reflect the zest people had for Jagjit Singh in Australia. The hall was bubbling with Indians all around, though few *firangs* could also be spotted here and there. The hall had round tables set up with ten chairs around each table, and although I did not count the exact number of tables, I knew there were enough to fill up this massive hall.

I looked at my ticket and found my table number. It was somewhere in the middle of the hall. Though I didn't like the view from my seat, I was happy to be there that night. Within some time, the concert began. Seeing Jagjit Singh live and attending his concert was too exciting for me. One after the other, Jagjit Singh sang all his famous ghazals, some from the movies and some from his albums.

I was thoroughly enjoying the renditions when suddenly my eyes fell on a boy who was seated two tables ahead of me, almost at a diagonal distance. I couldn't believe I was looking at Lee, or so I thought. That boy had the same face and the same features, but how could he be Lee? Wasn't Lee away from

121

Melbourne for a few days? At least that was what he had told me before leaving.

I started to recall the conversation I had with Lee when he had shared his travel plans with me in our apartment a week ago.

'Hey, Sushi, I am glad this Indian Film Festival is on now. You can watch as many movies you like, and that too for *free*.' Lee had said this while reading something from his iPad. He had stressed extra on the word *free* while saying this because he knew as students we hardly had enough money to indulge into fun things. We surely enjoyed our time and this phase of our lives, and we did things which weren't too heavy on our pockets; hence, this concept of free movies was alluring to most of us.

'Oh yes! It's going to be fun. I can't wait to show you some of these movies. I am sure you will have loads of fun too—if not because of the movies, then because of me at least.'

'Oh! I am sure, but only if you promise to watch some Chinese movies with me. I want to see how much fun you have while doing that,' Lee had retorted with a wink after which both of us broke into laughter.

'Yes, of course. We will see that when I drag you along with me. Oh, by the way, Sushi, I got a call from my one of my other friend this morning, and unfortunately, something urgent has come up. I might have to travel out of the Melbourne for ten days. I am sorry this is all happening now.'

'Oops! That's sad. Does it mean you will be missing out all these free movies?' I knew Lee didn't bother much about money because he came from a wealthy family. And he himself had worked before, so he had made some good savings.

'But don't you worry. If it's urgent, you must go. I will hang around with Kris and the others. Is there something I can help you with?' I had blurted out all this in one breath, perhaps feeling a little taken aback. I didn't want him to go, but I also knew that Lee wouldn't have planned to go if he could deal with whatever had come up by being here.

'Thanks, mate. But at this point, it's all good. You don't worry about anything. I would be gone for ten days, so I wouldn't be able to participate with you this time. But I promise I would be back soon, and we'll have a rocking time then,' Lee had replied immediately.

'Melbourne Central is just a walking distance from this place, so soak yourself in Bollywood films and sing, dance, eat, and enjoy your time. Once I am back, we'll have fun.' Lee added this not to sound too uninterested in Hindi films. Melbourne Central was a big mall in Melbourne CBD. Although from an Indian perspective, it wasn't really big. We had bigger and better malls in my city back in India, but with time, I had learnt to enjoy Melbourne Central equally. It was one of the most common meeting points for most of us, especially also because it had a big railway station in its basement with a food court which served our dual purpose of travel and food in one go.

'Are you sure you don't need anything?' I hesitatingly asked Lee.

'Sure thing, mate,' Lee replied.

'All right then. You carry on. I shall see you after ten days.'

'Sure,' Lee said with a smile.

This was the last conversation I had with Lee, after which Lee had left for the airport. I was now no more concentrating on Jagjit Singh or his ghazals. All I could think about was Lee and our conversations. I was feeling melancholic and betrayed and now uninvited to this concert, to this evening, and to this city. Everything seemed to make me feel unwanted. Why did Lee lie to me? Why did he go away so dramatically? My mind was full of these questions and more. I was angry with

Lee but more with myself for being so naive. I wanted to leave Melbourne immediately. I left the concert halfway through and made way to our apartment. By the time I reached there, I was less angry and more puzzled. I decided to confront Lee about all this and hence dropped my plans to do anything else. Lee was coming back on Sunday evening, which was just a day away.

Perplexed by the turn of events that evening, I decided to calm myself down and think about something soothing. I decided to watch a movie in my room on my laptop. With all the excitement of Jagjit Singh and shock of seeing Lee, I had almost forgotten that I hadn't had my dinner. So I got up and made some nice Maggi noodles in the common kitchen area of our apartment. Maggi has been my mood-lifter and a perfect cure for bad times ever since I had remembered. In fact, I could safely say that I was a Maggi baby.

But in Australia, I saw Maggi in a completely different avatar.

To begin with, it tasted nothing like the Maggi we get in India. The Maggi Masala of India was replaced with Maggi noodles in chicken, beef, lamb and pork flavours, and it wasn't even pronounced *Maggi*. It was rather called *Mai-ji*, which blew my mind in the initial few days of my stay in this country. Once bitten, twice shy, and so I never bought Maggi again from the Aussie grocery stores until I discovered the original Maggi from India which was sold in the Indian stores.

Anyway, leaving my Maggi saga behind, I began to watch *No One Killed Jessica*. I always liked watching suspense and murder mysteries. As the evening grew into night, I got lost into the movie and even forgot what had happened a few hours ago.

For now, I was really enjoying the hot Maggi and Hindi movie combination, but what would happen when I meet Lee on Sunday evening? Should I forget everything and spend a fun-filled time with Lee (after all, he has been my greatest support in this foreign country), or should I question him about his fabricated story? With these thoughts jumping up and down in my mind, I could not sleep even in the comfort of my bed and my blanket.

It was still 4.45 a.m., and I was wide awake with no signs of sleep at all. My mind was restless, just like my body. I constantly tossed and turned on my bed with my eyes closed, but it seemed as though the whole universe didn't want me to sleep.

Finally, I gave up all my efforts and got up to drink some water. I picked up the bottle kept on the floor next to my bed, but it was almost empty. I sipped on whatever water was left in the bottle and decided I needed something chilled, something more soothing, so I walked up to the kitchen, filled up a glass with cold tap water, and looked outside from the window while gulping down some water.

It was still dark, so I decided to dwindle some more time on my bed itself.

Not that I was scared of darkness, but the fact that it was windy and a bit cold outside made my bed appear more comforting than anything else at that moment. I walked back to my room and grabbed a magazine to read. It was difficult to say if it was the warmth of my blanket or the calming effect of the ice-cold water or the boring tales of magazines, but I had fallen asleep within minutes of being on the bed.

Sunrays seeping through the blinds fell directly on my eyes. I murmured something in my sleep and pulled up my blanket on my face. Then suddenly I threw my blanket aside and got up as though I had just been hit with something powerful, or maybe it was just the sun. I looked at my Samsung S4 to check the time and jumped with anxiety as it showed the time of 10 a.m. I had not realised that I had slept for another five hours after having water at the break of dawn.

I dashed into the bathroom and came out after a while, feeling fresh and clear in my head. I checked the time again and saw that the morning had slowly leaped towards noon, so I chucked the idea of having breakfast and decided to have some brunch instead. Before that, I made some instant coffee for myself and sat on the study chair in my room. I was not a coffee addict, but whenever my mind raced faster than my heart, the comfort of a hot drink always helped me to pacify that turbulence. Mostly, it would be a cup of hot chocolate, but on that day, it was coffee.

That day wasn't any different from the others. I felt great relief after having my *remedial* hot drink. I tried my best not to think about Lee. Though I was not totally successful, I was much better than the ghazal evening. I poured some cold milk over a heap of cornflakes which I had taken out in a bowl and ate it to my heart's content. The generous brunch and a cup of hot coffee had played its magic on me. I was feeling more peppy and happy than I had felt in the last couple of days.

It was half past one in the afternoon now, and having nothing much to do for the day, I thought of going online. I logged into Facebook and saw that there were no new updates for my profile. Those days, I wasn't very regular with the social networking sites, so my knowledge too was quite limited about what's happening in whose world. As I was browsing through the Facebook homepage, I saw a chat window popping up on the right hand bottom corner. It was a chat message from some old college mate from my school days with whom I was least interested in interacting, at least at that point of time, so I closed the chat window and thought of logging out of Facebook.

As I was clicking on the logout link, my eyes fell on Lee's profile. I wanted to ignore it, but something within me compelled me to take a peek at it. I clicked on Lee's profile and looked through his wall, just like a policeman who tries to fish out evidence before implicating the accused. My initial feeling was filled with guilt, but I also had a sneaking suspicion that I could find something to lash out at Lee. But Lee's wall was clean. It didn't have anything which could make me grow suspicious. I was disappointed with my efforts and skills.

Everything appeared normal, and I could not see beyond Lee's outer core into his real life. I felt exasperated and closed the Facebook window. Once again, I scanned my watch to check the time. It was quarter past three now. Time seemed to move at its own leisurely pace, which only added to my exasperation. I kept my laptop aside and switched on the TV for some entertainment.

The Big Bang Theory was showing on channel 9, and since it was one of the best comedies I had seen so far, I decided to stick to watching it. Quirky chemistry between the five friends, their constant snapped replies, and Sheldon's compulsive need to find logic in every word and thing in the world not only made me laugh but also gave me some occasional useful insights. The double-episode session was going on, so I was treating my mind to a good hour of laughter therapy.

If it was not for Einstein, the world would have never understood why each hour appeared like a second when you meet your lover or why each second appeared like an hour when you sit in a classroom. It was neither lover nor classroom, but for me, TV was a perfect example of theory of relativity of time, at least at that moment. Suddenly the intercom of our apartment buzzed. I jumped out from my seat and galloped to pick up the call.

'Hello,' I said with a little apprehension in my voice.

'Hi! Sushant. It's me, Lee,' said the voice from the other side.

'Oh yes!' I looked at my watch. It was six in the evening. The time had come for me to quiz Lee.

'Hi! Lee, come on in.' I opened the lift for Lee and hung up the intercom. Then I quickly went to the other room and switched off the TV. I didn't want to appear as if I was having fun.

A couple of minutes later, Lee entered the room. He was looking a bit tired but still had a smiling face and a bubbling enthusiasm in his voice.

'How was your Bollywood movie marathon, Sushi? I am so sorry I had to leave like this. But don't you worry, I have come now. I will make sure you enjoy every bit of your time here,' Lee blabbered in one go.

I felt the instinct to shout at Lee, but something within me stopped me from doing so. I looked at his tired face and decided to give him some more time. After Lee went into the bathroom, I sat in front of the TV and began watching my pet serial again. A couple of minutes later, Lee emerged from the bathroom and went towards the kitchen to make some coffee for himself. I looked at him and called him to sit in the common room with me, but Lee didn't reply. It was as if he had blocked his ears.

Perhaps he was ignoring me. I was almost certain he was. After a couple of minutes when he didn't reply, I walked towards the kitchen and tapped him on his shoulder. Lee shuddered with the sudden tap and turned back to see me standing. His eyes were moist and filled with tears. He immediately wiped them off and greeted me with a smile, 'Hey, sorry, Sushi. I didn't hear you coming.'

'That's all right. But why are you crying? Is everything all right?' I asked him with a concerned voice.

'I am not crying. Something must have gone inside my eyes.' Lee hurriedly wiped his eyes again and flashed his usual affectionate smile.

I took Lee's hand in my hand and squeezed it to comfort him. Then I hugged him and patted his back. Lee looked down in the dumps and not his usual self to me. *Something had surely unsettled him*, I thought to myself. I had known Lee as a strong boy, and it was shocking for me to see Lee unhappy. After some time, Lee turned towards me. 'I am sorry, Sushi. I didn't want to put you through all this, but I just could not contain this any more.'

'Don't worry, mate. It's all right to feel sad sometimes but not all right to suppress your feelings. Whatever it is, just blurt it out and get rid of the baggage,' I said to console Lee.

'You know that I had gone out of Melbourne for ten days. Well, it was not for work or to attend any urgent matter for a friend,' Lee started to pour out his heart to me, and I had also wanted to solve this puzzle.

'Alia, one of my friends, met with an accident two weeks before this entire film festival event in Melbourne. I went to see her a couple of times in the hospital, but since I was studying and working, I couldn't do more than that. She was doing well and was on her way to recovery. Two days before you spoke about going for the festival, I thought I would go to the hospital, and it being a weekday, Alia would get a nice surprise.' Lee's eyes swelled up with tears while recalling all these.

'When I went to the hospital, a guy was sitting next to Alia, and they were holding hands. After seeing me, Alia dropped his hand and smiled at me. I felt a bit awkward but didn't want to ask anything to her at that moment. She was getting discharged from the hospital that day, so I wanted her to be cheerful.' After saying this, Lee looked at me and saw the expression of confusion on my face. He understood what it meant.

'Alia and I had been dating each other for over two years now. We clicked instantly and were enjoying every moment of our relationship. Of late, we were going through some rough patches, but after her accident, I thought to myself that I will sort out all the differences,' Lee said, taking a deep sigh as if all that he said was meaningless.

'Then on the day when you mentioned the film festival, I got a call from Alia saying that she wanted to talk about something important to me in person. After her discharge, she has been living with her friends in Sydney, so I had no choice but to fly there.' Lee said all this with some guilt in his voice, or so I thought.

'When I reached Sydney, I straight away went to see her. She looked much better but still had her left hand plastered, and her face appeared pale. I asked her about what she had wanted to talk to me, but she said she will let me know and asked me to relax. I was totally lost. On one hand, I was thinking about you, and on the other, about her. I felt a little awkward being there, especially since Alia wasn't behaving how she used to be with me before. It felt surreal to me. Maybe that's because her friends were around, I consoled myself with this thought.' Lee grabbed the bottle next to him and gulped down some water.

While Lee's eyes were mourning the curtness of his beloved, his throat was selfishly craving for water. I couldn't ignore the irony of life at this point of time.

'Come, let's sit in the living room and discuss this over there,' I said to Lee.

Both of us motioned towards the common room and sat on the couch.

'Three days had passed, and Alia had not said anything to me so far, so I was planning on returning to Melbourne. But that very afternoon, she got a visitor. He was the same guy who was holding her hands in the hospital. He entered the house and hugged Alia. Alia gave him a quick hug but appeared visibly uncomfortable. She introduced him as Aan-sh, her colleague. I exchanged pleasantries with him.

'Later that evening, Alia said that they had five tickets for a ghazal concert in Melbourne, and Jagjit Singh was the main performer. She requested me to come along with her gang of friends. By now, I was deeply hurt by Alia's behaviour and was determined to return to Melbourne. If she already had plans to come to Melbourne, why did she call me to Sydney? So I thought I would go along with them and stay back in Melbourne itself.'

'Did Alia tell you for what she had actually called you to Sydney?' I asked impatiently. Lee was detailing every little part of his interaction with Alia, whom I later figured was his Indian girlfriend working in Sydney. I really wanted to help Lee, but I was getting a little restless with his descriptions. I did not have much choice anyway.

'No. She did not. I asked her on several occasions, but she kept postponing it by saying that it was something important, so she wanted to do that at the right time,' Lee replied. 'We flew down to Melbourne that evening and attended some singer's concert. It was a beautiful evening, and towards the end, I had almost forgotten about Alia's strange behaviour. After the concert got over, we were feeling very hungry, so we decided to go to some restaurant. We were five people, so we called for two cabs. Alia sent Aan-sh and her other two friends in one cab and sat with me in the other. I was feeling nice again. She held my hand and told me how nice I was and how much fun she had in my company.

'I was beginning to see the same Alia whom I had met two years ago. Then suddenly she said that things are not working well between us. Our priorities have changed and so have our feelings towards this relationship.' By now I could feel the wave of emotions swirling inside Lee. 'In two lines, she purged the very existence of our relationship and turned every sentiment into meaningless effusion of the human heart. She said I wasn't giving enough time to our relationship, and now she too doesn't feel the same way about me. Can you believe that, Sushi?' Lee said this and, without any breather, continued with his saga.

'So there was no point dragging the relationship for the sake of it. It was as if lightning had struck me out of nowhere. A sudden numbness had engulfed my soul, and I didn't know what to tell her. Alia kept talking to me, but I had stopped listening to everything around me. I asked the cab driver to stop immediately and got out of the cab. Alia held my hand and asked me to sit back. I freed my hand and got away from her. Before leaving, I asked her if she loved that other guy Aan-sh.

'She kept quiet and turned her gaze away from me. I understood. I didn't want to stand there any more, so I ran away from there.' Lee continued to sob while sharing all this.

'So where were you for the last few days? If you were in Melbourne, why didn't you come home, Lee?' I asked Lee with a surprise in my voice, which was a result of concern. All my anger and negative feelings for Lee had sublimed somewhere. I could feel my heart pounding for Lee's bruised heart, although I personally never had any relationship, barring few glances, some smiles, and occasional coffee dates at CCDs in India.

'I was too shocked and hurt at that time, Sushi. You were new to my world, and I didn't want to appear vulnerable before anyone. We had barely discussed much about each other's personal lives. Moreover, you had come here to have fun, and I didn't want to ruin that,' Lee replied.

'So where did you stay then?' I asked very softly.

'I went to another friend's house and stayed there till I could pull myself out from this mess. I know I should have come home or at least informed you . . .'

'Shhh . . . Don't say a word, Lee. I know what you must have gone through in the last week and how torturous the whole thing must have been for you. But I want to assure you that we are still the same friends that we used to be before this episode, and if at all anything has changed, then that has to be our understanding and bonding for betterment. You can still share your life with me. I am always here for you, mate.' I looked at Lee and said all this, dissolving any iota of coldness or strange feeling which these few days had created between us.

'You are a wonderful guy, and you certainly deserve to be with someone who really loves you and understands who you are. Forget Alia, and if required, give her a call to say thanks for freeing you up.' While I said this, I could see a faint smile appearing on Lee's face, and then we laughed it away like nothing had ever happened.

This was my first experience of seeing Lee emotional. The only other time when I had a glimpse of his emotional side was when I peeked through his diary and read his thoughts on his mom. Suddenly I had more respect for him now than I had before.

'I am so glad you are here. I promise you it will all be good now.' Lee said this and hugged me very tightly. I found comfort and assurance in Lee's company while smiling with relief, thinking that I hadn't lost my friend. As the saying goes, all's well that ends well. These couple of days were very disturbing for me, but at the end, I had got my mate back, and this time I knew it was for the better.

Both of us had suffered in our own ways in the days gone by, but now we had emerged closer to each other, and knowing that was just amazing. We promised to usher the coming days with total enthusiasm starting now and began discussing about our fun plans amidst unending chattering. This incident made me realize that relationships are indeed the same all across the world. Perhaps the only difference is in how we conduct them. Relationships are fragile in nature, and unless tested with time, one will not realize how much strong or weak it is.

I still remember my orientation day when I had gone out to buy a newspaper. I had coyly looked at the girl who was standing behind the counter at the newspaper stall, and my eyes were slipping over her silky smooth skin. I wondered what it would be like to have a girlfriend or even date someone in this part of the world.

Although I was never a champion in this area even back in India, whatever had happened with Lee had made me more apprehensive about relationships and its baggage. I wasn't sure whose fault it was in this case—Alia or Lee. All I knew was that I didn't like to see Lee sad and unhappy, and I certainly wasn't keen to see myself in that place either.

In India, I could not even think of holding hands with a girl and not worry about being reprimanded or shouted at by someone, while in Melbourne, holding hands didn't make anyone's muscle move. I had watched loads of English movies before, and in my mind, I knew how open the cultures were in the developed nations, but to see and experience that openness was another matter, something for which I took my own time to adjust.

The sight of couples kissing and hugging was common in trams, parks, shopping malls, and everywhere else, and so after my initial hesitations, these incidents seemed absolutely normal to me. I had pictured myself several times indulging into the same level of PDA, and every time, that thought had been washed away by the strong waves of self-doubt about securing a girlfriend—the chances of which seemed bleak to me with each passing day. Adding to that unassuming probability was the duration of my stay, which didn't leave me with much time to explore above and beyond my comfort zone. Other times, I thought it was good that I didn't have a girlfriend because I definitely could not splurge on our dates with my paltry part-time income. I thought of that girl I had bought my first newspaper from. She still appeared beautiful to me. My heartbeat increased a little, but I ignored it.

Whatever little opinion I had formed about people not valuing emotions in Western culture seemed to have blurred with time. People valued emotions and relationships just like they did in other parts of the world—especially in India, in my context. Otherwise, why did Lee look heartbroken?

I thought about my mother (who despite her awareness has a bias towards these people) and took a mental note of sharing with her what I had personally seen and experienced here—of course, just an overview, skipping any precarious details, lest she formed another set of bias.

Month 7

Chapter 12

Battle of Taste and Smell

I have come a long way since my inaugural adventure in the city of Melbourne. I have realised that no matter where we live, we will remain Indian all our lives because we like to remain Indian in our hearts and our souls. Fundamentally, it is not our love for our country which is responsible for this Indianness but more of our quirkiness which keeps this spirit alive—be it in Melbourne, New York, London, Germany, Kenya, or any other city across the globe.

During my journey Down Under, it also occurred to me that an integral part of our Indianness quotient was contradictions. For instance, we loved playing peppy English numbers in our car, but at home, we preferred playing the Bollywood chartbusters. My friend Kris was a perfect example of this case. If every evening we appreciated the Western sense of humour in *The Big Bang Theory*, *Friends*, *How I Met Your Mother*, and *Sex and the City*, every weekend, we also soaked up the cheeky, grand, and below-the-belt humour of our countless award shows, comedy shows, and grand soap opera sagas. We all displayed a little bit of Indianness in our day-to-day lives, although in varied degrees of equations, and I cannot deny being a part of such contradiction myself.

Such is the quality of Indianness that it gets rubbed on to us even without our cognisance, and it comes into play the moment we step into a foreign land, almost like our defence mechanism. It's contagious, it's conspicuous, and above all, it's irreparable. Some part of it has become immortal in the form of stereotypes, while others are yet to form a recognisable paradigm.

My Indianness always played its strong part at certain time in a year. It wasn't any different this time.

An unexpressed feeling of patriotism silently started engulfing my senses as the month of August kicked in. The Indian Independence Day and Republic Day are often those times of the year, every year, when I inadvertently got pulled back into the history of India. It wasn't any different when I was in Melbourne. Coming to the uni for classes on 15 August that year seemed like just another task in my daily schedule which took me down the memory lanes of my childhood where uncountable images of flag hoisting, national anthem's echoing, and faces beaming with pride kept flashing before my eyes.

I am not sure what it was, but since childhood, the Independence Day has had a mesmerising impact on my mind. As a kid, I used to love the adrenaline-pumping morning parades and other cultural events taking place in my schools, and although I have studied in nearly five different schools, the rituals on 15 August remained almost unchanged in each school. For me, the shift of school hardly mattered as the atmosphere on this day rang similar bells and the smell of the dust rising finely into the air with our parades felt nostalgic.

No matter how much I despised the parade practices during the school hours, the final parade on the Independence

Day always lit up my eyes. This eagerness and enthusiasm were further fuelled by the fact that on this day, we didn't have to open our books or sit in the classrooms or scribble down notes. What followed at home, post all the activities at school, used to be a lip-smacking spread of our favourite dishes which Mom used to prepare for us. This made us look forward to this day with acute excitement. The clarion of 'Vande Mataram' evoked an unexplained patriotism in my heart, which was further heightened by the sound of other patriotic songs played by people on their radios and music system from the break of dawn wherever we went.

As time flew by, we grew older and moved from the safe ambience of schools to the fascinating world of colleges, and we eventually stepped up to become an integral part of the multicultural student exchange programme. Amidst all this, the usual cultural activities and flag-hoisting got replaced with placid merrymaking, like catching up with friends and family over good food, listening to patriotic songs, and occasional indulgence in friendly debates on corruption.

The childhood emotion of doing something for our India was still intact in my heart, but the childhood liberation of expressing it had diluted somewhere along the timeline—a price we often pay for gaining maturity and worldliness. On such days when the entire India ate, drank, and smiled in merriment, the mere warmth of nostalgia helped those who lived far, far away from India in some foreign country for better lifestyles and paychecks.

Thanks to its multiculturism, places like Melbourne are inundated with Indians, and the feeling of being away from one's country is largely assuaged when you meet people from Kashmir to Kanyakumari and Gujarat to North East states Down Under. The Indian diaspora organised events and functions to celebrate everything from garba, kite-flying, Diwali, Durga Puja, Holi, to Karwa Chauth and Independence Day too, which filled our hearts with implicit emotions for India.

However, 15 August was one such day when my mind and heart transcended the political boundaries and visa requirements to stays in India, no matter how grandly and warmly one hoists the Indian flag at any event in Melbourne.

It is one such day when I like getting nostalgic over the sounds of 'Aye Mere Watan Ke Logon' and 'Maa Tujhe Salaam', an act which had now become a ritual for many fellow Indians in this land of opportunity.

Another occasion when my mind raced back to India was when my taste buds craved for some comfort food, and this happened quite frequently in my warming-up days. Melbourne is known as the food paradise of Australia, and true to its name, it is home to some of the most delectable cuisines from all around the world. Mexican, Italian, Indian, German, Moroccan, Ethiopian, Pakistani, Nepali, Chinese, Japanese, Lebanese, Afghani, Bangladeshi, Malaysian, Thai, Vietnamese, Sri Lankan, and others have conquered the taste buds of Melburnians and hooked them on to such varieties which are absolutely addictive. For me, this was particularly fascinating because back in my hometown in India, I wasn't particularly fond of such cuisines. I occasionally enjoyed Italian with my friends, but for most part of the time, it was Indian street foods, like *vada pav*, *chole bhature*, *paratha*, and *chaats*, which took my fancy.

During my initial few weeks in Melbourne, I survived on the known food items, and then on fast foods like Hungry Jack's, which was a blessing on students' pockets. It was only after I met Lee that I began tasting other cuisines, and I have to admit that I truly enjoyed this experience. We didn't have much money to splurge, so Lee, Kris, and I would pool in and choose one cuisine each time we could afford to eat out.

My favourite Indian food had taken a back seat in my life amidst so much of competition, mainly because I found the taste quite modified to suit the mild taste of the locals here. Over a period of time, I had developed a rather different perspective about taste and smell of the food.

Now, who doesn't like the smell of freshly cooked tandoori chicken or barbequed sausages with onion rings or deep-fried Kung Pao chicken, which yells hell with its fiery quotient? But imagine if you were asked to wear the tastes of these food items on your body as perfumes. Strange, isn't it? Well, not so much when you meet variety of people in this food paradise who truly believe in carrying their tastes on their bodies all through the day, much like wearing one's attitude on one's sleeve.

A large part of our happiness is driven by these two senses we tenderly call smell and taste. If a great-tasting platter can make us salivate, an intoxicating smell can certainly exhilarate our minds. Everyone loves to smell good and eat tasty food, but many of us end up enjoying either none or just one of these two. We've all heard about the saying 'Everything that glitters is not gold', and thanks to Melbourne, I have also realised that everything which smells good need not taste good and vice versa. In fact, taste and smell are like two sides of a coin, which are better defined when kept apart.

The aroma of fried garlic or stir-fried cabbage might turn the kitchen into a heaven, but some of us also needed to realise that such heavenly aromas can actually turn into nightmares for many noses when they step outside their kitchen. I am sure none of us would like our food to taste like, let's say, a Bvlgari Omnia perfume and our clothes to smell like salty fish-fried rice even though these are two great creations in their respective areas.

Sometimes I even felt like I had turned into some kind of fortune teller or clairvoyant who just knew what was being cooked in other people's kitchen. I mean, just one whiff of air was all I required to find out if someone had had a sumptuous chicken biryani for lunch or hogged on the mayo-laced cheesy and crunchy fast-food burger or relished a kangaroo steak or pork ribs for their dinner. Well, what's there to complain then? Although I love gorging on these dishes and enjoy their tastes to the core, I do not fancy smelling them, especially on other people's clothes and hair.

I got to witness this remarkable swap of taste and smell not only when I was visiting few of my batchmates' houses but also when I was travelling by trains/trams or in classrooms, in shopping malls, and almost everywhere else. Initially, I thought that this happens only with others, but soon reality bit me hard, and I did some introspection. While in some cases it might be difficult to avoid the food aromas from settling on our clothes and bodies, in most cases, we can prevent this from happening by simple common sense, provided we do a quick smell check before stepping out. A quick shower after cooking or at least a change of clothes, coupled with some use of perfumes, can go a long way in retaining the distinction between you and your food.

The post-lunch session in the class is another time when a great taste often gets butchered in the form of smell. Such times are especially distracting because while the mind is trying hard to concentrate on the sermons of professors, the nose gets busy ducking the smells from various cuisines emanating from various nooks of the classroom. What often makes the matter worse is the sheer ignorance exhibited by some people who believe that what smells good on the plate smells good on them as well. If the stench from the sweat is some people's nightmare, then the trace of fish and chips coming from coats, jackets, and shirts was my nightmare.

I had become so wary of the food smell that I had stopped wearing any jacket or sweater to restaurants. I certainly did not want to carry my food with me wherever I went because I truly believed that a great-smelling company can light up your mood and a delectable cuisine can fill your mouth with water and not the other way round. On multiple occasions, I had been tempted to inform a few students from my batch to leave the taste of the food in their mouths only and not transform it into a stench on their bodies and clothes in the common welfare of the rest of the people. Alas! I did not have the courage to translate these temptations into my reality, although to my friends I would often lie and say that I am being prudent and courteous to those people.

As the days passed by, my initial notion of freedom started becoming mundane as the feeling of liberation became a part of the everyday life. It wasn't until I left the cocoon of my awe, surprise, and excitement and stepped up to embrace the daily rigors of being an Aussie resident that I realised what other parameters defined independence in a country like this. Independence here meant the ability to make constant choice, whether you are at a supermarket, trying to buy just the right cornflakes for your breakfast, or at a coffee shop, trying to pick just the right strength, flavour, and aroma of coffee beans, from cappuccino, latte, flat white, espresso, or frappe! In the beginning, such spectrum of choice did get overwhelming on my mind so much that I hated it. However, subsequently, I started to see the underlying passion of people behind all these and understood that it was the freedom to make a choice and opt for what they like which made the sense of freedom so special and cherished to my heart.

Having a cup of coffee or a hot chocolate in Australia made me believe that size does matter; yes it does, at least Down Under. My lifetime understanding of small, medium, and large dimensions underwent huge metamorphosis after coming to Melbourne. And when I say this, I am not only talking about the size of people here but also about sizes of the clothes, fruits, vegetables, and anything else sold based on dimensions.

When I first landed in Melbourne, I was awestruck with the Aussie heights. Excluding the Asians, most of the people here stood tall with their towering personalities, and it wouldn't be wrong to say that I did feel like a midget with my 5' 10". I know it was stupid of me to think that way. Anyway, the only difference in my case was there was a large chunk of population which was even shorter than me in my class or uni.

However, this awestruck feeling soon turned into irritation and frustration when I realised that finding a pair of correct-sized shoes for me was almost a herculean task in this country, especially since I had noticeably small feet. Most of the shoes were either too big or too small for me until I took notice of my Asian mates and their feet sizes. I soon discovered several stores where I found shoes of my size in designs that I had always wanted to buy.

They had not only solved my problem but also bestowed some kind of solace to my sole . . . err, soul. And I too could say that I had a pair of happy feet!

Another instance when size struck me with its significance was when I entered the cooking domain like every new entry into bachelorhood. I wasn't particularly fond of cooking, but I sorely missed my mom's cooked food. It wasn't until one day when my cravings for hot and spicy food overtook my laziness that I took the matter in my own hand. My dreams of becoming a master chef got shattered when we were at Kris's house one day and my first attempt at making chicken curry went kaput.

The concept of one medium-sized onion and four flakes of garlic got totally messed up because, just like the people here,

Aussie vegetables are also huge in size. I used my Indian notion of medium, small, and large while exploring my culinary skills, and the resultant was a complete disaster. The proportions of all the spices got imbalanced which gave my chicken curry such a flavour that it got a unanimous thumbs down from Lee and Kris after tasting. It was only after several failed attempts in the kitchen that I could get hang of how much was too much. Until then, Lee and Kris had suffered many tasting disasters.

Like every successful scientist, I drew up my own conclusion. One Aussie eggplant is enough to satiate the taste buds of four people and whet their appetites too.

Trust me, it looks nothing short of a purple rugby ball. How can I not include cars in this mad tale of Aussie sizes? These automobiles actually look like fierce beasts racing fast on the long stretch of wide roads. The so-called small cars of Australia actually fell under medium-car segments in India. One of my personal favourite was Honda CR-V, which appeared majestic on Indian roads but looked like a small-sized 4WD on the Aussie freeways. I couldn't have believed it had I not seen it.

On various other occasions, I was reminded of the good old joke from my childhood where two people brag about the size of grapes and melons in their respective villages. It appeared to have come true all of a sudden. Soon it was to be my turn to brag about sizes when I returned to India, although there was a grain of truth in all these tales.

Chapter 13

Struck by Lightning

Just like a perfect story, while there were many fun moments, laughter, and great friendship that I experienced in Australia, there were some dark moments too which at that time felt like an unceasing journey of pain, fear, and uncertainty.

The glitz, glamour, and freedom of the developed countries can at times blur the thin line between right and wrong, especially for those who are new to this environment. There's been just one such incident which interspersed my otherwise fun-filled stint in Australia. It had been cold for a couple of weeks now, and we hadn't gone out much apart from commuting between our uni and apartment. Lee and I decided to break out of this monotony and experience the hustle and bustle of Melbourne nights. It was a unanimous choice; we wanted to go clubbing.

Lee had asked me to call up and check with Kris as well; however, due to our back-to-back classes, I just did not get time to speak to him. Lee had finished up early, so he had already left for our apartment to freshen up and change. I dashed out of the room as soon our class wound up. The evening was cold and biting, and it made me look forward to our fun evening plans with even greater fervour.

As I stepped out of the uni, my cell phone vibrated in my jacket pocket. I took it out from the pocket only to see 'Kris calling', and it suddenly made me realise that I had forgotten to inform him about this evening's plan. I knew Kris would throw some colourful words at me when I tell him that Lee and I made a plan without even informing him, so I was ready with my 'sorry' when I picked up his call on my phone.

'Hey, Kris . . . I am so sorry, mate. Almost forgot to—' I hadn't even finished my sentence when I heard a panicking voice from the other end.

'Sushaaantt . . . help me, dude. I am screwed.' Kris's words fell on my ear without making any sense.

'Hey, Kris, what happened to you? Are you okay? Why are you panicking?' I questioned him amidst lots of worries and confusion.

'I was caught by the police, Sushant. They are going to send me to jail, and they may even deport me back from here.' Kris was blabbering constantly, and I didn't know what to make out of that. So I decided to go and see him instead of talking on the phone.

'Are you at home, Kris?'

'Yes.'

'Great. Stay there and stay calm. I am coming over at your place. Do you want me to bring along Lee as well?' I told him to calm him down and also to make myself feel better. I had no clue of what was happening, and I badly needed Lee's expertise in this instance.

'Yes. Okay,' Kris murmured from the other end of the phone, or so I thought I heard.

I ended the call and quickly texted Lee to meet me at Kris's house. On my way to his place, I thought of all possible reasons or felony which could have put Kris in this situation. My imagination wasn't allowing me to go beyond what I had known him to be. What could have possibly happened to have landed him in such a soup?

Lost in my thoughts and confusion, I finally reached Kris's house. The house looked the same from outside, and it was difficult for me to even think that there could be some trouble brewing up inside it. After taking a good glance at the house, I finally knocked on the door and waited with bated breath for Kris to open the door. A couple of moments later, the doors opened, and I saw Kris standing behind it. He looked extremely petrified, and his face looked whitewashed with fear.

'What's the matter, Kris? What have you done? Why were you arrested by the police?' I immediately shot all these questions at Kris as I stepped into his house without giving him any opportunity to share what had transpired with him. I saw the exasperated look on his face and became quiet. My heart was racing very fast, and Kris's silence worsened my situation.

'Sushant, I am in a big trouble, bro. I just don't know what to do,' Kris managed to speak finally.

'Relax, Kris! You need to calm down and tell me what happened.'

'I was just sitting there, and it was kept right next to me. I smoked a little bit, and then the police came . . . and they took my mob . . . my mobile phone too.' Kris was hyperventilating, and by the mere look on his face, he justified a hospital admission.

'What where you smoking, Kris, and why did the police come? I am not able to understand anything. Please tell me from the beginning. I will obviously help you, but first, you need to tell me how all this started.' I had to intervene and get Kris composed to understand this situation. So far, he had only spoken in telegraphic codes and uttered some unrelated phrases, which were throwing me into deeper confusion.

'I had gotten down from the train at the Flinders Street station and was walking towards Southbank. I crossed the bridge, and while walking, I saw a packet with some herbs in it. It looked funny, but I went straight ahead. When I was coming back, I saw the same bench and the same packet on it. I became very curious, so I stopped and sat on that bench. That's when this happened.' He looked gutted.

'Why did you sit there, Kris? If you found that packet curious enough, you could have just looked at it and then left.'

'I wanted to leave, Sushant. You don't understand. It appeared very tempting, almost inviting to me.'

'So? I am clearly not getting what you are trying to say. What was it, and why do you say it appeared inviting to you?'

'I was smoking it, bro. It was a pack of marijuana abandoned by someone or forgotten by someone on that bench. I don't know how it got there.' These words had almost escaped Kris's mouth.

'What? Smoking marijuana? When did you even start smoking, Kris?' I was totally gobsmacked.

'I occasionally smoke cigarettes, Sushant. Lee knows about it, but I had asked him not to share this with you. It was a cold and beautiful day, and when I saw that packet of weed, I could not resist my temptation to get a taste of it.'

'Oh my god, Kris! What have you done? What were you even thinking?' I said almost feverishly.

Although it was just beyond my understanding how Kris could have done something like that, what astounded me more was that such acts were indeed seriously considered criminal offence in this country if caught red-handed. Back in my city, I had heard and also seen several boys from my college who would smoke joints. Some nasty ones would also inject themselves with obnoxious stuff to lose their sense and live in a world of illusion even though it meant only for a few hours.

Boys would hardly care if it was unbecoming of them. All that mattered to them was their fun.

Call it a lack of public awareness, social support, or courage, but I have only seen a handful of people tackling such addictions in a befitting manner.

I was still in a state of disbelief as though someone had just punched me in my stomach.

'Sushant . . . Sushant . . . are you listening to me?' I heard Kris's desperate voice in the background while he shook me from my shoulder. I saw him standing in front of me, totally shaken. This was one of those moments when nightmare begins after you open your eyes, and for me, the nightmare had just started.

'What are we going to do, Sushant? If anyone in my family gets to know about this, I will be dead.'

My brain was running fast. While still grappling with the thoughts of Kris amidst all this mess, I was also thinking about ways to get him out of it.

Suddenly there was a knock on the door. We both paused for a minute.

'It must be Lee. I had asked him to meet me here.' Kris looked at me with a blank face.

'I didn't know what situation you were in, and I wasn't sure if I could alone help you out, so I had to ask Lee to come over.'

There was another knock on the door so I rushed towards the entrance to let Lee in. As I opened the door, I saw Lee standing in front with his earphones in his ears and totally dressed in leather jacket and muffler to beat the chill outside, unaware of the thunderstorm and chill Kris had subjected us to. He was perhaps listening to music and thinking about having some fun time at Kris's place, blissfully ignorant of the tsunami which had rocked Kris's life.

'Dude! What took you so long to open the door? And where's Kris?' Lee questioned me, taking off his earphones as soon as he stepped inside. He looked at my pale face and immediately knew something wasn't right. I couldn't take all the pressure by myself, so I shared everything with Lee. I brought him up to speed with whatever I had learnt from Kris about this situation. Lee wasn't very amused to hear all this.

'What? Smoking stuff? Is this dude crazy? Did he not know it is not only wrong but also a criminal offence in this country? Moron.' Lee jumped up and down while vividly expressing his disbelief and perhaps some anger at Kris.

'I know it was stupid on his part, and he shouldn't have done it. But the fact is, he has already committed this offence, and the police are planning to press charges against him.' I wanted Lee to take off some pressure from me and not create some more. I was getting agitated as well.

I somehow managed to maintain my composure and decided to speak to Lee again. I touched him lightly on his shoulders and said, 'I know, Lee, you are a little angry right now and perhaps shocked too. I agree Kris has done a very wrong thing, something which you and I did not expect from our friend. But he is feeling very remorseful, shocked, and scared too. Whatever has to happen will happen, but you and I have to help him and support him in this ordeal. He needs us right now.'

'I know, Sushi. You are right. I just didn't expect this from Kris. He has lived here long enough to know what's right and what's wrong. Anyway, let's see how we can help him,' Lee said with a hint of exasperation in his voice.

'How big was that packet, Kris?'

'I don't know, Lee. It was a big packet. Must have been around half a kilo.'

'Half a kilo!' Lee almost screamed in disbelief.

'You are the most stupid person I have seen in my life. Who asked you to go even close to it, Kris? Had it been 50 grams and anything less than 100 grams, you could have still escaped. But you are totally screwed now.'

'I am sorry, Lee. I am sorry, Sushant. I didn't want to hurt anybody in this, including myself, but I know I have humiliated everyone,' Kris spoke for the first time since Lee's arrival in a choked voice.

'It was my stupidity, and now it can jeopardise my life, my career, and everything. I don't want to be called a criminal. Please help me.' Kris fell on his knees as he broke down and began sobbing profusely. I hadn't seen him hapless or crying ever before, so I just didn't know what to do. Should I comfort him and say everything would be all right when I have no clue what was going to happen next, or should I just stand there in silence till Kris regained his composure?

We looked at Kris. His face appeared distraught as though he was hit by an explosive force. I knew Kris, and I knew his zest for life. I could not see him in such a miserable state.

What began after this was a series of phone calls to various criminal lawyers across Melbourne. Every lawyer had different advice for Kris, but what was adding more stress to the entire situation was their legal fee, which ran in thousands of dollars. After dozens of calls and a few hours of deliberation, Kris decided to go along with Mr Mike Spector, who was an established lawyer in cases like Kris's, and more importantly, he was a *gora*.

'So it is Mike Spector! Are you sure, Kris, you do not want to go with the other Indian lawyer? He was in fact quoting you lesser fees as well,' I quizzed Kris.

'I am definitely worried about the amount of money I have to spend for all this, Sushant, but more than that, I want to feel confident and safe with the lawyer who represents me in this case. After all, my whole life is at stake.'

Lee and I looked at each other and nodded in affirmation to what Kris was saying. At times, I felt like giving him a piece of my mind, but then I would soon realise that was not going to help anyone of us in this situation. Although Lee and I were also going through lot of mental stress, we wanted to stand strong for Kris.

'Mike Spector has a higher fee, but he is a senior advocate, and I felt quite assured that he will represent my best interest. We have had lengthy discussions about the outcome of this situation if the police go ahead with the charge sheet, and I felt he was the only lawyer who did not lie to me, saying, "We will get you out of this." He was forthright and said, "We will do whatever needs to be done in your best interest." He discussed few approaches with me. I wanted to have a word with you guys before proceeding further.'

'We are certainly with you, Kris, and if you feel Mike Spector is best for you in this situation, then let's go along with him.' Lee looked at Kris and said this. He had a reassuring look in his eyes and a gentle smile on his face, which were what Kris needed at the moment. For a moment, I felt everything was all right in our lives again, but things were far from being okay. The nightmare wasn't over yet.

A few days later, I got a call from Kris.

'Hi, Sushant, how are you?' Kris said in a low tone. His single sentence utterance was enough to bring down the energy of the entire ambience.

'I am good, Kris. How are you doing?'

'Do you have some time to talk with me?'

'Sure, dude. Tell me.' I deliberately added some nonchalance in my voice to lighten up Kris's mood.

'I got a phone call from the police station this morning . . .'

'And?'

'And the police officer said that they have filed the charge sheet against me. This means my case will go into the court now.' I could sense high tension on the other side of the phone.

'Relax, Kris. Mike had already told us that there are high chances that the police will not thwart your case and file a charge sheet, so don't get worked up. We have Mike with us. He will guide us and help you overcome this, all right?'

'Yes, I know, but I can't help feeling scared and worried. What if they put me in the prison or perhaps deport me back to India?'

'I am shit-scared, Sushant. This is not I had dreamt about my life in Australia . . .' Kris broke down again before he could complete his sentence.

'Ssshhhh! Kris, please don't cry. We have talked about this already. You are taking more stress than needed. Did you tell Mike about your charge sheet?'

'Yes, I did.'

'Great. What did he say then?'

'He said my case is now undoubtedly going into the court for a hearing. He said to strengthen my case before the judge, I should get some stat declarations from friends and family.'

'Okay, and what does he want us to say in the stat declarations?'

'I will forward you the format Mike has sent me. It just says how long you have known me and how you have seen me as a kind and law-abiding person, and although I have committed an offence, I am extremely ashamed of it and sorry and that I should be given another opportunity to get my life back on track and . . . Don't worry, Sushant, I will send you the template.'

'That sounds good. Let's hope for the best, Kris. I know it's trying time for you, but all the more reason why you need to have a positive outlook right now. If we let our minds worry about the things and events which will unfold in the future, then when will we worry about things and events which are ready to unfold in our present?' I said this to pep him up while in reality I was pretty scared and sceptical myself.

'Will you also please tell Lee about all this? I will call him up later in the evening.'

'Sure, bro. Will do. Just don't worry too much.'

That evening, I told Lee all about my conversation with Kris and his lawyer's advice about collecting statutory declarations from his friends and family. Although I had known Kris for a very short time, I decided to write a stat declaration for him. It seemed like a time of reflection on my association with Kris. Memories are free from everything. They come without any warning, without invoking, and leave you even when you want to hold them tight and close to your heart.

Filled with nostalgia, I poured out my heart in the letter, outlining the strength of his character and his kind gestures which had helped people in need. I couldn't help but feel sad to see him distraught and in such a troubled situation. Lee also wrote a similar letter addressing to the judge, highlighting Kris's good qualities which he had experienced firsthand, perhaps more than me.

Next day, Lee and I went to meet Kris after our classes. The door was left ajar, so we entered his home after a single knock.

'Thanks for dropping by, guys.' A small smile broke out on Kris's face when he saw us. He was sitting on a chair facing the window. He had something in his hand. Perhaps a book. Bhagavad Gita, I assumed.

'Of course, mate. How have you been?' Lee asked while giving Kris a quick hug.

'I am good, Lee. How are you doing, Sushant?'

'I am good, dude. Take these letters. Lee and I have written what we thought was apt for this situation.' I handed over the printouts of the letter to Kris, which he immediately started reading. I was scanning Kris's face to see if he was happy with the letters or not. His forehead was drawn together which caused two deep furrows to appear right above his eyebrows.

I looked at Lee and signalled, asking if Kris was all right. Lee gestured his hands down, indicating me to be quiet so that we don't disturb Kris. After nearly five long minutes, Kris shifted his gaze from the letters and looked at me and Lee and hugged us both together.

'Thanks a lot, guys. I am just overwhelmed reading your letters. I knew we were good friends, but I never knew you guys thought so highly of me. I am even more ashamed and mortified of my act now. I have not only breached an important law of this country, but I have also shattered your faith in me. I have caused too much agony in everyone's life who is attached to me, but I promise that I will work double hard if needed and mend all broken hearts and resurrect my principles and ethics. I love you, guys, a lot,' Kris blurted out all in one breath and let out a sob before getting back to himself, or so I felt.

'Of course, we know that, Kris. Let's try to put this in the past and try to build your future,' Lee said in a very reassuring tone, and this was the major reason why I got him involved in this case. I knew I could rely upon him to pull Kris back from this mess.

'When is your hearing?'

'It's tomorrow.'

'Shall I come with you? I can bunk a few classes and be there for your hearing.'

'No, it's not required, Lee. Thanks you so much. I had a word with my lawyer today, and he said it was best for friends

158

to stay away from my hearing. So I guess I will have to be there alone.'

'Oh, okay. Don't worry, Kris. If your lawyer has advised it, then let's follow that. We will be available on the phone all through the day, so give me or Sushi a ring as soon as the hearing gets over,' Lee told Kris.

'Sure, will do, bro.'

'Has Mike told you your chances of not getting convicted in this case?' I quizzed Kris.

'Mike said there can be four outcomes—I may get deported out of Australia or I may get a twelve-month imprisonment with criminal conviction or I may be asked to pay a fine with criminal conviction or I may not be charged with any criminal conviction but may have to perform certain hours of community service in addition to being fined.' Kris shared mechanically as though he had memorised these outcomes for some university exams.

'Mike said he will try to get me the community service option. But I don't know.' His positivity had stench of relinquishment.

'That sounds really good, Kris. Please don't get disheartened before the hearing is over. Mike must have thought of something before saying that to you, so just keep your calm, get a good night's sleep, and go fresh for your hearing tomorrow. We will pray for you.' I smiled at Kris while saying the last sentence to him. I wanted him to feel as positive as he could. After nearly thirty or forty minutes later, Lee and I decided to leave and go back to our apartment.

As scared as we were, it was important for us also to take a rest as we had to attend our classes amidst this entire hullabaloo and yet feign all the time as though nothing wrong was going on in our lives. Perhaps for the first time in my life, I was beginning to feel reverence for the actors, who toiled in various conditions and got into the skin of characters as if it were really them. I was finding it hard to pretend for a little while also.

Next day, I got up with the ring of my alarm. I opened my eyes, shut it down, and realised that I wasn't really sleeping. The thought of Kris and his untold future kept me up the whole night. I tossed and turned all night, but sleep seemed miles away from me. I looked at my cell phone again to check the time and pulled the blanket on my face to snooze for some ten minutes.

Those ten minutes were weighing too heavy on me, so I decided to get up and get ready. Lee was already in the shower by then, so I too hurried and freshened up so that I could go to the uni with him. Anyway, I wasn't able to focus much today as my head was filled with thoughts of Kris and his impending uncertain future.

It was around one thirty in the afternoon when Lee's phone rang. It was Kris's call. Lee picked it up but could not hear anything. Both of us dashed out of the class, and this time, I rang up Kris.

'Hello, Kris, what happened? What did the judge say?' There was silence on the other end. I was not sure if Kris was able to hear me or not, so I repeated myself, still unsure.

'Hello, Kris . . . Are you there? Are you able to hear me?'

'Hello . . . Hi, Sushant . . . Yes, I can hear you,' Kris said in a hush-hush voice.

'Tell us what happened. Why are you hushing?'

'Oh, I was still in the court premise, that's why I was speaking slowly. My hearing is over. There was a lady judge, and she criminally convicted me. I also have to pay a fine of $3,000.'

'Oh, okay. So does it mean you are not going to the jail or getting deported?'

'Yes, that's right. No jail time and no deportation. However, there will be a criminal offence registered against my name, and I may perhaps not get an Australian citizenship.'

'That's it! It is such wonderful news, dude. We are so happy—' Lee snatched my phone even before I could finish my sentence.

'Kris, Lee here. Dude if I heard what Sushi was saying, then it is great news. Imagine what we all feared just a day ago. You are free now. This calls for a party. We don't want to listen to anything. You come to our uni now, and we will discuss and celebrate this good news our way, just like the old times.' Lee sounded very happy, and I too couldn't contain my excitement. It now felt like a nightmare which had at last disappeared with the night—a very long and a very bad one.

Finally, the ordeal seemed to get over. We were desperately waiting to celebrate this occasion with Kris and get him out of his misery.

While this entire episode was oozing chaos and panic-stricken reactions, I learnt some crucial things about this faraway land. If this situation had occurred in India, Kris perhaps might have been able to escape by throwing away a couple of thousand bucks and pulling some strings here and there—but would he have understood the gravity of damage done to himself, to us, and most importantly, to his own character?

The painstaking process in Australia was daunting and gruesome, but I was sure, along with Kris, we had all learnt our lessons and realised that law is equal for all. I knew at that point that this incident will remain as one of the highlights of my life Down Under for all its ups and downs and also for bringing to the forefront the testament to the most withstanding relationship of our lives—friendship.

Month 8

Chapter 14

Home Beckons

Amidst all the rigmarole of my so-called lifestyle in a developed nation, what solaced my heart most was the excellent curriculum at the university, my impressive performance, and some really great friends who helped me sail through whenever I grappled with the eccentricities Down Under. It was a different matter that in those few months I had become Sushi from Sushant and learnt the famous Aussie alphabetical swap between *A* and *I*, which made the word *mate* sound *might* to others.

I still had two months left, of course, after which I had to return to India for my final exams, and I had complete plans of unravelling the reality of my Aussie lifestyle to my friends there.

One thing which would certainly cheese off my American mates and some Indian and European folks too would be the no-tip culture of Australia. When people render bad service to us, you not only feel like not giving them any tip, but you also feel like deducting from their fee just to express your dissatisfaction. However, when someone overwhelms you with a great haircut, mouth-watering food, neatly trimmed nature's strip, or a well-dry-cleaned dress, you feel like rewarding them with over and above their stipulated fee, right? Ah! That's where Aussies again bowled me over with their no-tip culture. Be it in restaurants, hotels, or toilets, Aussies do not accept and encourage tips, so I made no efforts to please them with this antic. It's a different story that as a student I never felt I had enough money to tip anyway.

How many of my friends' *whoa*, *wow*, and *amazing* turned into 'No way', 'You gotta be kidding me', and 'Really!' is another big tale which can be penned down into a separate book. For most of them, I would just be a killjoy of their peppy and glamorous NRI world, which has been skilfully concocted by the likes of Chopras, Johars, and Khans of our Hindi film industry over the decades.

So this was the first chapter in the story of my life, which I will cherish forever. Whatever I learnt and experienced in this multicultural country is absolutely priceless, perhaps because neither any book nor Google could have translated these life experiences to me in any better way than what I went through.

It has been seven years since the day I first landed in this country, but it still feels like it was just yesterday when I was filled with trepidations. Since then, I have learnt more about the people and culture of different countries than I have learnt from the books in my class. While there are things which are still beyond my comprehension and cognisance, there are other things which have enriched me as a person and helped me develop a wider perspective in life.

Over these seven years, I had travelled several times between India and Australia, and now as a Melbourne-based NRI, I have experienced some unique situations which can be better termed as being on the other side of the coin. From being a teenager who met his NRI cousins in India to becoming an NRI, I have realised how biased we have been to our cousins.

Callous wind, perpetually grey skies, unpredictable rain, incomprehensible love for footy—phew! These are just few of the things that can irritate a person who steps into this much-hyped city, tendering dreams of a luxurious life. Dreams do get fulfilled in due course of time, but in this mad rat race, the newly turned Melburnians often jostle through numerous doses of these daily tortures. Along with playing home for some of the world's biggest sporting championships, Melbourne also hosts hundreds of thousands of immigrants who come here in search of a better life, and I wouldn't be surprised if Melbourne earned the name Immigrant Valley in the near future! A country which was once the other world for me has now truly become my own world.

What began as a sojourn of exploring an unknown territory and a chance to create new dreams ended up becoming a package of some beautiful moments, some eye-opening revelations, and a plethora of heart-warming memories for a lifetime. The last seven years have been very instrumental in shaping up my life.

From my initial feeling of irritation to getting used to the Aussie anecdotes, this city gradually grew upon me, and now I feel a certain bond with it, which appears inexplicable to me at times. Now I feel nostalgic about every single aspect of Melbourne, especially on the days when I am away from the chaotic and harebrained comfort of this city often crowned as the Most Liveable City in the world.

Little did I know that a strange country and some strange faces would form an integral part of some of the defining moments of my life.

The somewhat shy teenager of India had gradually evolved into a much confident professional of Australia who had embraced the immigrant-rich circle of friends here even if it meant he had to transform from a peaceful and a calm person into a much-loved food from Japan.

'Sushant, Sushant, where are you?' I heard Avantika's voice in the background.

'You are still standing here, Sushant? Hold this. Lee's on the other line. I have already wished him a happy birthday.' Avantika almost said this like an announcement and handed over the phone to me. She took away the empty cup of tea I had been holding in my hands, perhaps almost sensing the memories and thoughts which had flooded my mindscape for so long ever since I woke up this morning. I didn't even realise when I got pulled back into the past while still standing on my balcony and watching the morning metamorphose into a beautiful afternoon in Melbourne.

'Happy birthday, mate. I was just thinking about you and me and Kris.' A smile inevitably broke out on my face as I wished Lee a happy birthday, reminiscent of our wonderful years in Melbourne.

The grey clouds hovering over our building had finally scattered now, and I could see the sunrays shining warmly over my head as I heard a voice from the other end of the phone, 'Sushi, how are you mate? Aa-vi wished me before you this time.'

'Of course she did, Lee. After all, she knows you are my best mate.' And with this, both of us got engrossed in yet another heart-warming conversation about our lives and some fun planning for a great reunion to relive some of our good old days spent in the times of Melbourne.